"The Wate   Just f

The moonlight glittered on Dan's bare chest, cast mysterious shadows over the dark planes of his face. He shed his trousers, then his shorts, and stood before her naked. So strong. So male.

Mutely he extended his hands to her and she found herself stripping off her own clothes. Then he was taking her hands and leading her to the water's edge.

The whole thing was like a dream, she thought, this little oasis in the middle of the desert. In some far-off corner of her mind she knew she should be frightened—here in this strange place, in the mysterious moonlight. But there was no fear in her. She trusted Dan.

NORA POWERS

taught English at the college level while working on her Ph.D. A prolific writer, she is the author of some 500 pieces of children's verse, 58 short stories, 9 novels, and various newspaper articles. She has been a published author for the last twenty years and reports, "I don't even recall how I started writing, I was so young."

Dear Reader:

SILHOUETTE DESIRE is an exciting new line of contemporary romances from Silhouette Books. During the past year, many Silhouette readers have written in telling us what other types of stories they'd like to read from Silhouette, and we've kept these comments and suggestions in mind in developing SILHOUETTE DESIRE.

DESIREs feature all of the elements you like to see in a romance, plus a more sensual, provocative story. So if you want to experience all the excitement, passion and joy of falling in love, then SILHOUETTE DESIRE is for you.

I hope you enjoy this book and all the wonderful stories to come from SILHOUETTE DESIRE. I'd appreciate any thoughts you'd like to share with us on new SILHOUETTE DESIRE, and I invite you to write to us at the address below:

Karen Solem
Editor-in-Chief
Silhouette Books
P.O. Box 769
New York, N.Y. 10019

NORA POWERS
In A Moment's Time

Silhouette Desire
Published by Silhouette Books New York
America's Publisher of Contemporary Romance

Other Silhouette Books by Nora Powers

Affairs of the Heart
Design for Love
Promise Me Tomorrow
Dream of the West
Time Stands Still

 SILHOUETTE BOOKS, a Division of Simon & Schuster, Inc.
1230 Avenue of the Americas, New York, N.Y. 10020

Copyright © 1983 by Nora Powers

Distributed by Pocket Books

ISBN: 0-671-47202-X

First Silhouette Books printing August, 1983

10 9 8 7 6 5 4 3 2 1

America's Publisher of Contemporary Romance

Printed in the U.S.A.

For Miriam,
without whom I would
never have seen Old Vegas

1

Abby Holland pushed a strand of black hair off her forehead and stepped down from the tour bus, suitcase in hand. It had taken her a little while to convince the bus driver that she only wanted to go one way. After all, he had his orders. If he arrived at a place with twenty-six passengers, he expected to depart with the same number. Unless, of course, they didn't return to the bus by the designated time, as he had so explicitly warned them.

Most of the visitors to Old Vegas—the recreated Old West town with its cantina, photo shop, candy store, silversmith and other shops—just came for the day. Abby was there to work on a publicity brochure for Old Vegas and she planned to spend a month or so at the tourist town doing research.

She could have rented a car, of course, for the drive out from Las Vegas, but she really had no use for it. The tinsel and glitter of the Vegas strip had no appeal for her. She'd seen it all last year. It had been gaudy, flashy and empty then. It would be the same now.

Only now she had no need even for the distraction. Last year she'd been in a state of semishock, hurting so badly that she hardly knew what she was doing. Any place had been OK then, any place away from Art and his hateful words.

As the bus pulled away, Abby looked around and began walking toward the wooden cantina. The atmosphere of the Old West that had been so carefully reconstructed in Old Vegas was lost on her. Instead, her mind was full of that last painful meeting with Art. How could she have been married to a man for five years and known so little about him? It seemed incredible now, incredible to think that she had not even suspected his duplicity. He had been cheating on her for almost a year; he had told her so on that fateful afternoon.

He had found what he'd been looking for. He wanted a wife—an old-fashioned, stay-at-home, nothing-else wife. Something Abby had never been.

In her hurt and bewilderment she had sought answers, but Art had had none to give her. Except that he was tired, he said, of a wife who was always out on assignment; he wanted his dinner on time, his pipe and slippers waiting. This new business of partners was not for him. It didn't work.

He wanted a divorce—he wanted it immediately. And in the end, there had been nothing to do but give it to him. She had tried to protest—had even asked for another chance—but Art refused. They were no good together, he said harshly. And that was that.

8

Abby stepped into the coolness of the cantina, a welcome contrast to the heat of the sun. She grimaced slightly at the ever-present sound of the slot machines. Even here people had to gamble.

She looked around and finally spotted the manager's office. As she moved toward it, she heard the town sheriff calling the tourists to gather around him. A faint smile curved Abby's generous lips as she raised her hand to knock on the manager's door. The sheriff looked his part: guns slung low on his hips, Stetson pushed back on his head (though perhaps his stomach was a little more ample than necessary).

The door opened at her second tap. "Ms. Holland." The manager's smile was bright. "It's good to see you."

"Thank you, Mr. Seccord. I'm glad to be here. I hope to do a good job for you."

"I'm sure you will. Come in, come in. And sit down. I'll fill you in on whatever you need to know."

Abby settled herself in a wooden ladder-back chair. "Thanks. I think I have a pretty good idea. If possible, I'd just like to wander around."

Jim Seccord nodded. "That's OK by me." His friendly face broke into a grin. "But there's been a new development. Are you familiar with *Vacation Today?*"

"Of course." Abby nodded. Who didn't know the name of the most prestigious travel magazine in the country?

"Well"—Seccord seemed about to burst with enthusiasm—"they want you to do an article in addition to our advertising brochure."

Abby barely stopped herself from clapping her

hands, managing a more restrained "I'd be glad to do that." She smiled slightly. What an understatement!

Jim Seccord nodded, his smile indicating that he knew what a plum this was for her. "I've assigned you a trailer. The people who work at Old Vegas live here. Some of them, anyway." He waved a hand in the general direction. "I've given you a place to yourself. I imagine you'll need some privacy to write." He gazed at her speculatively. "How long do you think it'll take you?"

Abby leaned back in the chair, intent on this job, all thoughts of Art erased from her mind. "I've allowed a month," she said. "It may take a little longer now, with the article. Maybe six weeks or two months."

"That sounds fine." Jim Seccord pushed absently at his horn-rimmed glasses. "I've lined up our photographer for you. He runs the photography studio here. Folks can go in and choose a costume, then have their picture taken."

Abby nodded.

"Name's Dan Jenkins. You'll like him."

Abby got to her feet. "That'll be fine, I'm sure. Now, if you'll just point me toward the trailers, I'll get settled in."

"Of course." The manager stood up and accompanied her to the door. "I'll send Dan over. Say in half an hour. It's trailer number six." He handed her a key.

Abby stepped out into the cantina. The smell of cooking food assailed her nostrils, reminding her that breakfast had been some hours before. Too many hours. But she didn't want to be dragging her luggage around, and Mr. Seccord would be sending the photographer over. She'd just have to wait a little longer, she told herself, as she moved through the interior of the town.

It was much as she remembered it—weatherbeaten wooden buildings surrounded by stockadelike walls. Dust puffed up from beneath her pumps. She moved slowly, ingoring the tourists and the chattering children, evidently visiting on a school vacation.

Her first visit here had been very different, urged on her by a well-meaning friend who had first suggested Vegas as a suitable place to forget Art. She had not noticed much at first, numbed as she was. But gradually the spirit of the place had reached her. There was something different about it, something far more intriguing to her than trying to beat the one-armed bandits that infested the hotel lobbies like some kind of encroaching alien race.

A smile curved Abby's mouth. There she went again, letting her writer's love of words carry her away. At any rate, her first visit to the old town had been followed by a second and a third. She liked watching the eager faces of the children as they helped the Sheriff track down and capture Black Bart, the bandit. The person who had dreamed up these dramatizations certainly had been creative. Abby had thought so on her previous visit, and she thought it again when she heard a voice come over the loudspeaker announcing that in ten minutes there would be a "shoot-out" in front of the jail.

Yes, the town had taken her fancy on her first visit. Contrary to her usual practice, she had inquired at Sutler's Store for postcards or a descriptive pamphlet. Her surprise at being told that nothing like that existed had prompted her to seek out the town's manager and offer her services. The idea had appealed to him, but since the owner of Old Vegas had been out of the country, Abby left a proposal and her address. Six months passed before the absent owner had returned and given his approval. And six more before Abby could work the trip into her schedule.

She suddenly realized she had passed Hard Rock Pete's candy store and was trudging down the trail to where the trailers clustered, hidden from sight unless one looked out from the parapets up on the stockade wall.

Number six was small—definitely not luxury accommodations, Abby told herself with a slight laugh. But it did have a small air conditioner and all the necessary furnishings: bed, table, chair, a tiny kitchen and bathroom. It would do quite well, she thought, as she put her bag on the freshly made bed. Now to wash her face. It might still be March, but this was Nevada and the middle of the day—and the sun felt hot, especially to someone who had just left Pittsburgh's ice and snow.

She was drying her face on the clean but somewhat faded towel when there was a tap on the door. Towel still in hand, she moved to open it.

The man who stood there was tall—six feet at least. Eyes that were almost black sparkled at her from a darkly tanned face. Curly black hair spilled over the collar of his old-fashioned black frock coat and out from under the derby perched rakishly on the back of his head. His nose was bold and roman, presiding over a bushy black moustache. Abby stared in fascination at that moustache—a long, black handlebar moustache—as old-fashioned as his clothes.

"Well, hello." His voice was deep and smooth.

Belatedly, she realized that she was staring. "Hello."

"I'm Dan Jenkins." He grinned, revealing white teeth. "Dapper Dan, the gambling man."

To her surprise Abby found herself grinning too. "I'm Abby Holland."

He nodded. "Besides my erstwhile role as Dapper Dan, I'm the town's photographer."

"Of course, Mr. Jenkins." Abby was suddenly flustered. "I'm sorry, I'm not quite oriented yet."

"That's OK. That's why I'm here. Jim Seccord asked me to work with you. Give you any help I can."

"That was very kind of him," Abby replied. "And of you."

For some reason she was reluctant to ask this man into the trailer. The quarters seemed so small —and he was such a big man.

He returned her gaze, his frankly appraising eyes traveling over her beige pants suit. "Have you eaten?" he asked finally.

Abby's breath came out in a whoosh of relief. The tension in the little trailer had seemed tremendous. "No, I haven't. And I'm famished."

"Then let's go over to the cantina and get a bite to eat. If you came in on the tourist bus, you've got a free meal coming anyway."

"How . . . how did you know I came that way?" she asked.

He shrugged his broad shoulders. Her mind registered them automatically.

"I don't see any car out here." He looked around him at the sandy soil and the occasional clumps of tumbleweed. "And it's too far to walk and too expensive to take a cab." He looked down at her low-heeled pumps. "You look like the practical type to me. Also, you've been here before."

His eyes met hers with a warm friendliness that was unnerving, but she dismissed the slight uneasiness in her mind. He had taken her by surprise, appearing in costume like that—and looking so much the part.

Involuntarily, her eyes moved to his hands and a chuckle bubbled up in her throat.

His gaze followed hers and he laughed, a warm pleasant sound. "Yes," he said, holding up his left hand. "I wear a pinkie ring. Helps me fit the part. The diamond's not real, of course. Nothing's real around here. It's all one big make-believe."

He glanced upward at the sun. "Now, if you don't mind, can we get some lunch? I'm beginning to feel kind of silly standing out here."

Abby felt the blood rushing to her cheeks. She hadn't blushed in years, she thought in wonderment. "Of course. Just let me get my purse."

Minutes later she stepped down from the trailer, pulling the door shut behind her. He reached a hand out to steady her; she felt its warm pressure momentarily on her elbow. "Better take my arm," he suggested with cheerful friendliness. "This sand can be treacherous."

Abby shook her head. "I'll be fine, thank you."

Dan's sigh was large and exaggerated. "Don't tell me I've got a liberated woman on my hands."

She knew he was joking, but the subject held no humor for her and the sharpness of her tone told him so. "I don't disdain help when I need it, Mr. Jenkins. But neither am I a weakling who needs constant care."

One of his heavy black brows shot up and he frowned. "Sorry, guess I hit a nerve."

Her reaction had been much sharper than he deserved and she knew it. "I'm sorry too," she said. "That subject is a sore spot for me."

"I'll accept your apology if you'll accept mine." His smile had returned and she wondered if he knew how attractive it made him. "Agreed," she murmured.

"So you're a writer."

Abby nodded. "That's what my tax form says. And you can't fool the IRS."

"What kind of stuff do you do?"

"Oh, things like this. Publicity brochures, pamphlets, in-house stuff. Freelancers take what they can get. Did Mr. Seccord tell you about the *Vacation Today* article?"

Dan nodded. "Yes. And from his enthusiasm I gather it's rather important."

Abby laughed. "Not just rather. *Vacation Today* is *the* vacation magazine. Just wait until the article appears. This place will be overflowing with tourists."

"That important, huh?"

Abby's expression was eloquent. "That important."

Dan pulled thoughtfully at his moustache. "Seems like I'm going to get some of my pictures in a pretty classy mag. How about that!"

Abby was spared answering this rather rhetorical question since they had reached the cantina. She pushed the door open before Dan could reach it for her, but once inside she had to pause. Coming in from the sunlight like that had made everything very dim.

She felt Dan's hand on her bare elbow, felt warm, strong fingers, and a little tremor shivered along her backbone. She dismissed it easily enough, telling herself she was tired—and it had been a long time since an attractive man had touched her.

She allowed him to guide her up the broad wooden stairs to the cafeteria line. The tourists who had come in on the same bus with her had finished by now and were outside, wandering around the town, taking pictures or buying souvenirs at Sutler's Store.

Abby loaded her plate liberally. Breakfast in the plane seemed ages ago, and although it was only lunchtime here, her stomach was still following a Pittsburgh clock.

"This OK?" he asked as they settled at a table across the room.

"Fine," she replied, turning her attention immediately to the food.

Ten minutes later she sighed and pushed away an empty plate.

"Feeling better now?" he asked, wiping his moustache on a napkin.

"Oh, yes. Much better."

Abby's reply was so heartfelt that he laughed. "Then we can talk business."

She felt a flush of embarrassment. It was strange how this man could fluster her so easily. Ordinarily she was unflusterable—if such a word existed. After all, she was used to working with all kinds of people, including very important ones—actors, artists, prominent executives. Well, she didn't have time to worry about it. She had a job to do.

"Of course. Here's what I had in mind." She reached in her purse for pad and pen.

Half an hour later Dan took the notes she offered him. "I think I've got the idea." He looked around the nearly empty cantina. "Want to come over and see my shop?"

Abby shook her head. "I know it's only midafternoon, but I think jet lag has crept up on me. How about a rain check?"

Dan pulled a gold watch from his vest pocket. "I have three o'clock. How about four-thirty?"

Abby laughed. She hadn't meant to, but there was just something about this man that disarmed her. She heard the warnings in her head, warnings that had originated with Art's betrayal. And, of course, she had no intention of becoming involved with any man—not intimately involved. In business men could be dealt with, but in personal relationships they changed. They became strange creatures who wanted not a real, live woman—not a person at all—but a possession, an object, a "thing." And she had no intention of becoming a "thing" again.

Art's betrayal—for that's what it was to her—had been a horrible shock. Hadn't they talked about her career before they married? And hadn't he agreed that it was just as important to her as his career was to him? And then the truth had come out—after five years of lies. The truth that he had never really wanted her to have a career, had thought she would eventually settle down and become an ordinary housewife.

"Four-thirty?" Dan Jenkins repeated. "We might as well start with the photo shop."

Abby nodded. "Sure." The man was right. She had to see the entire town in order to write about it. Besides, if she saw the photo shop today, then tomorrow he could be off taking pictures and she could be attending to her business—alone. Already she was aware of it—the insistent physical pull of this man—an attraction she hadn't felt since the carefree days before her marriage. An attraction she definitely did not mean to pursue. Not today or any other day.

2

~~~~~~~~~~~~~

The nap left Abby feeling more rested, but she did not feel more at ease about Dan Jenkins. This project was not going to be the semivacation she had envisioned when she took the job, she thought, as she stepped into the tiny shower. First, an article for *Vacation Today*, whose editor had eagle eyes, was quite a different story from a small advertising brochure or a descriptive pamphlet. Still, she was a professional; even though this was her first article for the prestigious glossy, she knew she could handle it.

The second problem was not so easily surmounted—she could not discount Dan Jenkin's very real physical appeal. In her personal relationships she was definitely not a professional. Witness the stupidity with which she'd continued in a marriage which she hadn't even recognized as dead. She was no longer sure what irked her more—the end of her relationship with Art, or her naivete in thinking that all was well—when it wasn't. At any rate, she thought as she stepped out of the shower and toweled herself vigorously, she wasn't going to allow herself to be hurt like that again. Dan Jenkins could be as friendly as he liked; their arrangement was going to be strictly business.

The sun was still shining brightly outside the trailer's small windows as Abby got dressed, selecting a gaily flowered skirt, a white peasant blouse and sandals. She was well aware that she presented a very different picture now than she had on her arrival, but the beige pants suit and black pumps had served their purpose. She had established herself as a businesswoman. Now she could be comfortable.

She considered putting gold hoops in her ears to complete the Mexican look of her outfit, but decided against it. She had chosen these clothes for comfort and ease in packing, not for making herself attractive. And she certainly didn't want Dan Jenkins to get the idea that she was trying to please him.

For a moment this idea almost made her return to the little closet and her pants suit. Then she shook her head, realizing she was being ridiculous. She wasn't going to be uncomfortable simply because of a man. She grabbed her shoulder bag and started out for the photo shop.

Warm sand trickled into her sandals and gritted under her toes as she made her way up the slope toward the town. She was glad to be where it was warm. Pittsburgh winters could be mean.

This part of Nevada was certainly barren desert, she thought, as a dried tumbleweed rolled past her.

She remembered her initial surprise at the sight of the plant the year before. For some reason the West had meant prairies and mountains to her, not these vast stretches of sand supporting nothing but sage-brush and tumbleweed. But of course they were as much a part of the West as the rest.

As she walked up the slope, the outer part of the town became visible to her. She sent a momentary glance to the railroad car. No doubt its regal interior had once housed some big Eastern banker. Abby smiled at her thoughts. Her mind was always taking these historical tangents, going off on flights of fancy about long-gone people.

This was a part of her, she thought as she crossed the sandy square, and probably one of the reasons why this place appealed to her as it did. Art had accused her of refusing to grow up, but she didn't think that was true. He was the one who had wanted the old-fashioned wife. And anyway, didn't experts say that it was the childlike part of people that inspired creativity? She never wanted to lose the part of herself that could look at the world with joy and wonder.

By this time she was passing through the inner gates and into the stockaded part of town. She sent a curious glance at the stage for the medicine show as she passed. She'd never quite managed to catch one of the performances there, and she looked forward to it.

The door to the photo shop was open and she paused outside, more than a little nervous at facing Dan Jenkins again. She did not like this kind of feeling. It interfered with her functioning as a writer. She wanted to stop it.

"Well, hello there." Dan had removed his black

frock coat, but the brocaded red vest and the gleaming garnet cuff links in his white shirt sleeves still proclaimed his "fancy man" role. He ran a hand through his unruly hair. "I've been awaiting your arrival with bated breath."

Abby couldn't help smiling. It was hard to resist a man who made such graceful fun of himself.

"Won't you step into my parlor?" he asked, extending a brown hand, the one that flashed the fake diamond.

An unexpected giggle bubbled up and out of Abby's throat. "Said the spider to the fly?" The words were out before she could stop herself and she saw from his delighted look of triumph that he had anticipated her reply—in fact had been angling for it.

"I suppose I might qualify as a spider," he replied with a gracious smile. "But you are far more delectable than any fly."

"Thank you, kind sir." Abby decided that the best idea was not to take him too seriously. She would play along with his little game and keep it that—a game. After all, there was no harm in some fun. She'd had very little of that for some time.

She managed to avoid his hand as she stepped into the shop, but she could not forestall its coming to rest quite firmly under her left elbow. For a moment she considered pulling her arm away, since the contact was far too pleasant and therefore distracting. But she decided that it might be better just to ignore it. Dan Jenkins looked like a man who was used to charming women. If she were too standoffish, he might see her as a challenge that had to be met. And she could certainly do without that kind of complication in her life.

"Do you do much of a business here?" she asked, consciously turning her mind to her assignment.

"Enough," Dan said, his eyes on her face. "But let me show you around."

The hand under her elbow moved her easily forward to where an old-fashioned straight-backed chair stood before a backdrop.

"Here's where they sit. The man on the chair and the woman standing slightly behind him—her hand on his shoulder."

Abby felt a swift stirring of indignation. "In her proper place."

Dan's look was quizzical. "We do it the other way too, sometimes. Depends on what the customer wants." A broad sweep of his hand indicated the adjacent wall. "See?"

Abby turned to look. It really was a good idea, she thought, as she examined some of the photos. Some photo shops took pictures of people standing behind cardboard bodies, bodies of anything from a harem dancer to Mickey Mouse. But Dan's photos, done in a sepia tone, looked genuine—as though they were really old.

"It must take a lot of costumes," she said.

Dan shook his head. "Not really. We have several gowns in each size, a few dress suits, some cowboy clothes."

A spirit of mischief tugged at Abby and she grinned. "What if a woman comes in and doesn't want to be cast in the role of dutiful wife?"

Dan's hand slid down from her elbow to her fingers in one swift motion and before she could protest he was pulling her toward the back room. "I'll show you."

There was no time to try extricating her hand, for suddenly he came to a stop by a rack of clothes. "This is the ladies' dressing room." He grinned. "In case you hadn't guessed."

Abby's swift intake of breath was automatic. Green velvet predominated over bright blue as well as drab pioneer brown. The sight would have gladdened the heart of Scarlett O'Hara. "Where did you get them?"

"Most of them are re-creations," he said. "We hired a dressmaker and sent her to the museum. Most old garments are too fragile to endure such constant handling."

Abby nodded, her eyes still on the gowns. Her hand went out automatically to caress the material; its richness appealed to her senses in a way she had not experienced for a long time.

"You like those?" His voice was warm and he was standing entirely too close.

Abby felt the fine hair rising on the back of her neck, little ripples of excitement shivering down her spine. "I—yes. I've always liked the past."

She spoke to the clothes, not to the handsome face so near her own. If she turned her head just a little, she would find those dark eyes gazing down into hers. And she knew instinctively what she would find in them. Once she would have welcomed the sight of desire in a man's eyes, but now she knew more. Now she knew that men were not to be trusted, especially the charming handsome kind who were used to wrapping women around their little fingers.

"What is it about the past that fascinates you?" Dan asked, his voice becoming lighter and less intimate, almost as though he had sensed her thoughts.

Abby moved sideways along the rack of clothes, ostensibly examining the gowns but actually trying to put more room between herself and this disturbing man. Her forehead wrinkled as she considered his question. "I don't know exactly. Except that it seems grand. And beautiful. Richer." She paused and turned to face him now that he was not so close. "There's more color to the past. More substance."

"More excitement," he volunteered, his wide mouth curving in a smile.

Abby smiled too; she couldn't help it. "Maybe. But not just that. There are exciting things going on today. Space travel, computer technology. But the past has something else, something more. Elegance. Charm. A sense of fitness."

"Excuse me," Dan said, "while I go find the lady a soapbox."

Abby's laughter pealed out. "I didn't mean to preach. I've never really tried to put my feelings into words before. It's just that the past has always intrigued me. When I was a little girl on my way to the library I used to go by stately old houses with hitching posts still out front, and I'd imagine beautiful ladies in long gowns promenading around."

"You're a pretty beautiful lady yourself," Dan said, and again his voice dropped to that intimate, inviting level.

Abby chose to ignore it as well as the invitation in his eyes. "Where are the men's things?"

"In the next room," Dan replied. "I'll show you in a minute. But first I want you to see something else. Just the gown for you, since you object to the role of dutiful wife." His eyes examined her face briefly as though looking for a clue to her earlier behavior, but Abby had herself in hand now and her face remained calm.

"This is what the well-dressed dance-hall girl wore." He pulled a costume off the rack and extended it to her.

Abby couldn't help herself; she knew that her face lit up. The dress was of bright red velvet trimmed with black ribbon. Its bodice, which was clearly designed to fit tightly, was cut low with little ruffled straps over the shoulders. The skirt, reaching the floor, was narrow, with a bustle in the back.

Dan grinned. "You wear it with black stockings and a red feather in your hair. But, of course, you would know that."

Again Abby's laughter pealed forth. She hadn't laughed much this last year. "Do you have many takers?"

Dan's grin widened. "Only from unescorted women. Here, try it on."

Again Abby felt the unusual color mounting her cheeks. "Oh, I couldn't."

"Of course you can. I bet this is just the right size too. Come on, slip into it. I'll take a shot of you. There's nothing like experience to add authenticity to your copy." His eyes caught hers and she found herself holding her breath.

He was right, and Abby knew it. Besides, she felt an almost childish delight at the prospect of seeing herself in this daring gown. She reached for the hanger in his outstretched hand, giving in even though the warning voice in her head was starting to awaken.

"I'll be waiting in the front," Dan said, his eyes regarding her warmly. "I'll take a picture you'll keep for a long time. Now you can be one of those ladies you used to imagine."

His fingers brushed hers as she took the gown from him and the surge of emotion that pulsed through her almost made her cry out from its intensity. He felt it too, she knew, for he looked down into her eyes for a long silent minute. Her knees quivered beneath the flowered skirt and she tightened her grip on the hanger so that he wouldn't see the sudden trembling of her fingers. The pull between them was strong, so strong that for a moment she thought he would cross the small distance separating them and take her in his arms. But the moment passed and he gave her a brief smile as he turned toward the door. "I'll be waiting."

The door closed behind him with a snap and Abby stared down at the gown. Then, before she could feel any more frightened than she already was, she began to pull off the flowered skirt and the blouse. Her bra had to be discarded too, she saw. The gown did not allow for it.

With fingers that still shook she slipped the gown over her head. It fell to her hips with a satisfying rustle, and a sigh of contentment came floating from her lips. There *was* something about these clothes; they gave her an intensely feminine feeling. She smoothed the tight-fitting skirt across her hips, smiling as she did so. The fit was perfect.

Slipping her arms through the little ruffled straps, she pulled the bodice up. It was constructed so that when laced up the front, it supported her breasts— or that part of them that remained concealed, she thought wryly. There was a good deal of their rounded smoothness exposed. Evidently, the dance-hall girls had no qualms about advertising their wares.

For a moment, as she stared at herself in the full-length mirror, she considered backing down. The gown made her appear seductive, which was not exactly the way she wanted Dan Jenkins to think of her. That would complicate their business relationship. But the appeal of the gown was tremendous. Some childish part of her was gleefully pleased at the picture she presented, and she wanted the photo that Dan had promised her. She wasn't sure why, or what it meant to her, but she did know that she wanted it.

And anyway, she told herself with a toss of her head as she reached for the feather, other men had found her attractive. That didn't mean she had responded to them. Or that she would respond to Dan Jenkins.

Digging briefly in her shoulder bag, she came out with a handful of hairpins. Deftly she twisted the long coil of her hair, securing it on top of her head and adding the feather at a jaunty angle. A fresh application of lipstick and she was ready. Best to get out there before she lost her nerve.

Dan turned as he heard the opening of the door and his quick intake of breath sent warmth through her whole body. "Wow!" He said the word softly, with reverence. "It looks like it was made for you."

"Thank you." She brushed nervously at the skirt. His glance was too admiring. She wished now she had not agreed to this foolish idea. She was a grown woman; she shouldn't be playing dress-up games, especially when they made a very attractive man's eyes linger caressingly on her partially exposed breasts. "Could we take the picture now?"

"Of course. Right over here." He motioned to the chair. "Do you want to stand or sit?"

Abby seemed unable to think. He was just too close, too overpowering. "I—it doesn't matter."

"Leave it to me," Dan said as he took on the manner of the professional photographer. It was a manner designed to put a person at ease. But it failed to work for Abby, primarily because she could not forget the warmth in his eyes—or the answering warmth in her own body.

He led her before the backdrop. "Stand here."

She followed obediently, her only thought now to get this over with. How could she have knowingly gotten herself into such a situation?

Dan backed off and looked at her critically. "Turn a little to the right."

Abby did so.

"Put your left hand on your hip. That's it." He grinned. "This is going to be an extraordinary photo. I may even add you to my gallery over there."

Abby felt the color flooding her cheeks. Why hadn't it occurred to her that he would keep a copy of this photo?

He continued to study her for a moment, his look so intense that when he suddenly stepped toward her she almost lost her pose. His fingers touched her chin, gently, softly, and she felt it clear to her toes.

"Tilt your head like this," he said softly, his lips only inches from hers.

Abby tried to control the sudden mad beating of her heart. It was the costume, she told herself. In her own clothes she would not have felt so vulnerable to this man's maleness.

"There," he said, considering the effect. "But your eyes are wrong. They're too soft, too warm. Women like this were supposed to be hard."

"I suppose they had feelings too." Abby's reply came quickly and automatically. "If it didn't make the men hard, why should it have affected the women?"

One of Dan's dark eyebrows shot up. "I did it again," he said with a rueful grimace. "I insulted you when I meant to compliment you. I guess I'd better get a book on dealing with the liberated woman."

"I'm not insulted." The words slipped out before she could stop them and she hurried on to explain. "I just hate the double standard and I say so whenever I see it."

Dan nodded. "I respect that."

He was still only inches away and her senses quivered with his nearness. The scent of his aftershave—tangy, with a hint of something she couldn't quite define—assailed her nostrils. He was so close. He had only to reach out and . . . She drew back from the thought. The last thing she needed now was a romance. "The picture," she reminded him.

His eyes lingered on her face for another moment before he nodded. "Of course. Just hold that look." He backed away, buried his head under the black cloth of the old-fashioned camera. "Now." The light flashed.

"Wait," he called as she started to turn away.

"We need several shots. Turn this way. That's it. Moisten your lips. Good." The light flashed again.

"Now. One more. Put your other hand on your hip. Look provocative. Think of a man you've loved."

The pain was swift and sudden, so sharp and unexpected that she had no defense against it. She had loved Art, loved him a great deal.

Dan's head emerged from under the cloth and he took a swift step toward her, almost as though he meant to comfort her. Then, seemingly thinking better of it, he backed off. "Tilt your head the other way. A little more. That's good."

She knew that he had seen that flash of pain on her face. And, tactfully, he didn't mention it. For that she was very grateful, especially since a lump had formed in her throat and tears were shining in her eyes.

"That's it," he coaxed her, his manner all business. "Now smile. You just heard you got the *Vacation Today* job."

His tactics were obvious to her, but they worked nevertheless. The smile that appeared on her lips was genuine. Dan immediately darted back under the black cloth. Again came the flash of light.

He emerged smiling. "That should do it. You make a good subject. You should have been a model."

Abby's chuckle was nervous. "I'm a writer."

Dan nodded. "I know, but you could have been a model. You've got the looks for it."

Abby shook her head and tried to achieve a light tone. "Flattery will get you nowhere, sir. I warn you."

But Dan didn't smile in return. "It isn't flattery.

31

I'm speaking the truth. The honest truth, Abby."
His eyes held hers for so long that her mouth grew
dry and her palms wet.

"I-I'd better change."

"There's no hurry." His words were soft, meaning much more than they said. She knew that, and
she did not know how to respond.

"I-I'll be right back," she stammered.

His eyes followed her as she hurried from the
room; she felt the heat of them as she closed the
door behind her.

She returned a few minutes later, hoping she had
herself in hand. She glanced at him nervously.
"Thank you for the guided tour."

"You're quite welcome." His voice still held a
caress; she could feel it.

"I-I think I'll go back to my trailer and make
some notes."

Dan pulled the old-fashioned watch from his
waist coat pocket. "OK. It's five-thirty now. I'll be
there around seven."

"What for?" She hated the tremble in her voice.

"I thought we could have dinner in town." His
smile was charming and little-boyish. "The cantina's food is good, but you'll be getting a lot of it. I'd
like to take you to dinner. A nice little place in
town."

Abby shook her head. "No thanks. I'll settle for
whatever the cantina's serving."

He crossed the distance between them and she
barely kept herself from backing away in panic.
"Come on, Abby, relax a little. You know what they
say. 'All work and no play makes Jill a dull girl.'"

Those dark eyes were very appealing and for a
moment Abby considered giving in. She wanted to.

The time she had spent with him had been very pleasant. But she shook her head again. He was a man and she had vowed to deal with all men on a strictly business basis. She was not ready to become someone's "thing," someone's possession again. She would never be ready for that. "No thanks, Dan." She turned quickly toward the door. "Thanks again for the tour."

She heard his "Abby, wait" as she pulled the door shut behind her, but she didn't heed it. She didn't dare.

3

~~~~~~~~~~~~~~~~~

The days passed. Two days, three. Abby saw Dan often, more often than she would have liked; the pull was still there between them, the magnetism that made her want to forget all her resolutions.

He presented her with a copy of the photo of herself in the red gown, appropriately done in a sepia tone and framed in an antique oval. "Thank you," she said. "I don't know what else to say."

"It's a lovely picture," he replied. "A good addition to my gallery." He smiled. "You look very real."

Abby nodded. "I know. I can hardly believe that's me."

"Maybe it's the real you," he suggested softly. "Or a part of you. How about dinner tonight, Abby?"

"No thank you, Dan. But I do like the picture. Thank you again."

She turned down two more dinner invitations after that, but he did not seem offended. She almost wished he were. It would have complicated their business relationship, certainly, but that could not have been any more tension filled than it already was.

Over breakfast with Jim Seccord on Thursday she discussed the progress of her work. "I really like the dramatizations," she said, sipping her coffee.

Jim nodded. "I think they're fun. In fact, we've decided to add a new one and we're trying it out today. Dapper Dan gets shot by Black Bart; Lizzie, the dance-hall girl, comes running to help her man."

Abby had visions of the red velvet gown and felt a quick stab of something very like jealousy. "Who's going to be Lizzie? I don't recall seeing any women in your other dramas."

Jim nodded. "We haven't been using them. Till now." He pushed his glasses up the bridge of his freckled nose. "I think this is going to be a big draw. Lizzie is going to be played by Nan Sherwood. She works in one of the saloons."

Abby set her cup down absently. She remembered the girl, about her own size, but with short blonde hair. "I see. And Dan and Black Bart are already regulars."

The manager nodded enthusiastically. "I told Dan it was a great idea."

"What has he got to do with it?" Abby's tone was sharper than she liked.

Jim Seccord looked startled. "He plays a part in it. Of course I talked to him about it first."

"Of course." Abby softened her voice. She tried

another tack, a more indirect one. "Where did the idea come from?"

"We've been thinking about it for quite a while. I asked everyone to try to come up with something new."

"And who came up with this?" She knew she was pressing, but she had to have an answer.

"Dan and I worked it out between us." The manager frowned. "I don't think this kind of thing is going to have a lot of interest for readers of the brochure."

Abby hurriedly recalled herself to her assignment. "I like to know everything I can," she said. "A writer never knows what information will come in handy."

The manager did not look convinced and Abby couldn't blame him. She knew quite clearly that the reason behind her questions had nothing to do with her assignment here. But why had Dan suggested such a skit? Had her appearance in the red velvet dress given him the idea?

She would never know; it was not the sort of thing she could ask about, for she knew instinctively that to do so would immediately put them on a level of intimacy that she could not afford.

"Abby!" Jim's friendly face was still worried and she realized that she had not been listening to him.

"What? Sorry, Jim. I was thinking about my article."

The little lie soothed him even if it didn't make her feel any better. She felt a flash of distaste for herself. She was using her career as an alibi—and she didn't like it.

"I said, we'll do it for the first time at two this afternoon in the square."

Abby smiled. "I'll be there, of course. It should be very interesting." She finished the last of her coffee and put down the cup. "Now, if you'll excuse me, I'd better get back to work." She forestalled the question she saw coming with a gracious smile. "Yes, I'm moving right along. I should be done well before the deadline."

"That's good." He stood up as she rose from her chair. "And Abby, if you have any ideas for skits I'd be pleased to hear them, real pleased."

She let her smile grow broader. "Sure, Jim, but drama is not my thing, you know. I'm strictly a reporter, a journalist—not a novelist." Not that I wouldn't like to be one, she added silently. But that was a private dream. "See you later."

The morning passed swiftly. With her notes and Dan's photos spread out before her on the trailer's kitchen table, Abby smiled in satisfaction. Everything was beginning to take shape. She was confident that this brochure would be one of her best efforts.

The article for *Vacation Today* was something else. There was plenty of material—no problem there. But the angle to take, the special approach that would make this something more than a collection of written facts—that was what she needed. And that was what she didn't have—yet. She sighed and pushed a lock of hair back from her forehead. The little trailer's windows were open and the early April sun, though warm, was not uncomfortably so, but she felt suddenly far too hot.

She glanced at her watch and noted to her surprise that it was just after one. After she got a light lunch it would be time to head for the square and Dan's new drama. She was positive that the idea had been his. This certainty gave her two very different sets of feelings, she realized, as she stepped into the tiny bathroom to rinse her face. On the one hand, she found it disturbing that an idea like this should have grown from her photo session with Dan. It surely indicated that the incident meant too much to him. On the other hand, though, some small part of herself was absolutely glorifying in this very same fact. It was all too confusing, she thought, drying her face. Confusing, and not at all conducive to finishing the job she had come here to do, or the revisions on a previous article that were waiting to be finished.

With a sigh she moved back toward the door. She wasn't particularly hungry, but the body was a machine like any other and it would not run without fuel. The next time someone went into the city she would have to go along and get a few groceries. Then she could prepare something light for herself instead of always eating at the cantina.

She had just reached for the doorknob when a sharp rap on the door made her jump and jerk it open.

"Hello, Abby."

It was Dan who stood there. For a moment her heart pounded, but she forced her voice to be calm. "Hello, Dan."

"Listen, Abby. We've got a big problem." His eyes were full of worry and his brow crinkled in a frown. Only then did she notice the garment bag hanging over his arm.

"Nan, who was going to play the dance-hall girl this afternoon, well, she just got sick. Upchucked her lunch. And I thought of you. . . ."

Her heart rose up in her throat. "Me? What do you mean me?"

"You're just the same size. You can take her place."

Abby's head moved automatically in a no. "No, Dan. Not me."

"Don't be silly. You know you can do it." He hurried on, ignoring her gasp of dismay. "It's your chance to play at make-believe. A real chance." His eyes pleaded with her. "Come on, Abby. Just this once."

"But—I don't know the lines. I can't." Silently she acknowledged to herself that she really wanted to do it, that all her protests were fake.

"There are no set lines," he said. "Bart and I argue. He shoots me in the shoulder. You come running up and bandage it with a strip from your petticoat. We had one made up from cheap cloth. It's in here, along with the dress."

"I can't," she repeated. "Wait till Nan gets better."

Dan shook his head. "She's sick because of the skit. Stage fright. There's no time to get anyone else, and we can't wait either. The owner's coming around just to see it. If he likes what he sees, Jim and I get raises and the chance to plan some more skits. Please, Abby, it won't take long."

She stared at him, torn by her conflicting emotions. She knew doing this would be very dangerous; it was playing right into his hands. But he was clearly in need of her help, and he *had* done a great deal of work in the shots for the article.

In the end neither of these arguments swayed her, but, instead, a very real—though she was afraid childish—delight in the chance to dress up and play make-believe. Almost of its own volition her hand reached out for the garment bag. "All right, Dan, I'll do it. But just this once."

"You're a real sport." His grin reflected great relief. "You don't know how much this means to me. Go to the Arizona Club, the saloon, when you're dressed. The action takes place out in front. And thanks again."

He was gone then, striding off toward the stockade, little spurts of dust puffing up from beneath his black boots.

For a moment Abby stood still. This couldn't be happening to her. Then a sense of excitement swept over her, and she pushed all the reasons why she shouldn't be doing this out of her mind and hurried into the bedroom.

When she emerged from the bedroom some minutes later, she looked like another woman. She felt like one too, she conceded, as she stepped down to the ground and set off toward the town. She had donned the red velvet dress and black stockings, adding her own high heels. But she had done more than that. Her brightest lipstick outlined her mouth and she had applied both eye shadow and rouge with a liberal hand.

This whole thing was madness, of course; she ought to have been back in the trailer working. But what she had said to Jim Seccord that morning had held a certain amount of truth. There was value in having information. There was also value in having experience, as any good writer would readily affirm. And one never knew just which experience would prove most useful.

She held the gown up out of the dust as she moved off toward the town square. It felt strange to be walking around in a dress like this. The sun was warm on her bare shoulders and she felt a moment of panic, but it receded quickly. She was really not doing anything so terribly outrageous, and the dress was decent enough by modern standards.

She suppressed a smile as she passed Hard Rock Pete's and grew aware of the wide-eyed stares of two six-year-old girls. "Look!" One nudged the other. "Look at the lady!"

Abby had drawn even with them by this time and she allowed her smile to appear. She was instantly rewarded by two returning ones.

As she crossed the square, several men stepped out of the big jail cell set prominently there. She did not quite understand why anyone would want to have a picture taken in "jail," but many people seemed to. Someone was always waiting to be next.

She stepped up on the boardwalk and entered the Arizona Club. Several girls were behind the counter serving cold pop. Nan Sherwood was not among them. "How's Nan?" Abby asked one of the girls whose saloon-girl costume accentuated her small waist.

The girl shook her head. "She left a while back. Got sick, you know. You gonna be Lizzie?"

Abby nodded.

"Well, I wish you luck." With a cheerful smile the waitress moved on to serve another thirsty customer.

Abby turned to look out at the square. Today there was a busload of children from an area school. What a fun field trip the kids must be having, she thought. And what a pleasant way to learn the history of their state. The children were scattered throughout the town, eager voices chattering over the marvels they discovered. There was also a good sprinkling of adults, some with small children in tow, some older and alone, and several pairs of hand-holding teenagers. It was a good crowd, though a noisy one.

The sudden blaring of a voice over the loudspeaker reduced the sound of the crowd to a mere whisper. "Ladies and gentlemen, this is your sheriff speaking. Now if you'll just proceed to the town square, you'll be in time to see Black Bart up to his villainous tricks."

Abby's hands had grown damp as he spoke. She must be crazy. She couldn't do this in front of all those people. What was she doing dressed like this? But she had to do it. Dan was depending on her. She wiped her hands again, nervously, and moved toward the front of the saloon.

The curious tourists had begun to gather, clustering on the boardwalk in front of the stores, men whispering to their wives, mothers calling to their children.

Then she saw Dan. He was wearing his black frock coat, but it was unbuttoned and his red brocade vest showed. His dangling watch fob and diamond pinky ring caught the sun and sparkled. He looked every bit the part, she thought absently. From his black boots to the angle of his rakish hat he was the picture of a "fancy man."

A sound over by the railroad car seemed to catch his ear and he started. He turned—and so did all the spectators—to see Black Bart come striding from behind the car. "Stop!" Bart yelled.

Abby's hands moved nervously over the hips of the red gown. The newly constructed petticoat was already cut to make ripping a piece off easier. That was kind of melodramatic, she told herself. But then the whole thing was sheer make-believe anyway. And everyone knew it.

The argument between Dan and Black Bart grew louder and a hush fell over the crowd. Abby's heart pounded in her throat. Soon now.

Dan shook his head. "You're a poor loser," he said and the words carried through the silence. "I don't cheat at cards, Bart. I don't need to." He turned his back on the irate villain and walked away.

A collective gasp rose from the throats of the crowd as Bart drew his six-shooter, but Dan was oblivious to it. He moved nonchalantly on toward the saloon.

Even though Abby expected it, the shot made her jump. Dan stopped, clutched at his left shoulder, and crumpled slowly to the ground as Black Bart jumped on his horse and galloped off over the ridge.

The sheriff rode out from behind one of the buildings and took off after him, leaving Dan to lie in the dust.

"You better go," whispered a voice beside Abby, but she was already halfway to the door. Then she was out of it. "Dan!" The cry that was wrung from her was so real, so full of anguish, that it startled even her. Then she was running awkwardly across the dusty square in her high heels, the red velvet dress clutched in her hands.

She reached his side at the same moment that he pushed himself to a sitting position. "I'm all right, Abby. He just winged me." His words carried to the waiting crowd.

She was so much into her part that the substitution of her name for Lizzie's hardly registered.

His hand came away from his left shoulder, revealing a spreading red stain. Her sound of dismay was authentic and it took his whispered "Easy, Abby, it only looks real" to make her realize that he had been holding something in his hand, some kind of red liquid.

"You could smooth my brow or make some kind of sweet gesture," he said under his breath. Automatically her hand went out to push the damp hair back from his forehead.

"Sit still," she commanded and, turning her back on him, she lifted the red velvet skirt far enough to rip off a piece of the flimsy petticoat. She saw now why the black stockings had been necessary. "Here, this'll do till we get to the doctor."

He pressed the wad of material to his shoulder and reached for her hand. "If you just help me up, I can walk."

It was crazy, some distant part of Abby cried, but the whole thing felt real, especially her concern for Dan. It was as though some strong bond existed between them and even an imaginary threat to him affected her.

With her help, he got to his feet. For a moment he leaned on her, actually leaned so that she could feel his weight. "I'm all right, Abby," he repeated. And she almost forgot that the words were meant for the listening audience, not just for her. Then suddenly he was drawing her to him with his free arm. She forgot everything then; he gave her no chance to protest before his lips claimed hers.

She did not fight him. She told herself that it was because of the role she was playing, but she knew

44

better. She did not fight him because she wanted that kiss. She had wanted it, probably on a level unknown to her conscious mind, from the first moment she laid eyes on him.

His lips were soft and persuasive and hers opened to him just as her body pressed willingly against his, unheedful of the pressure of his arm. It was a brief kiss; he was conscious of the spectators even if she were not. Slowly his mouth left hers, touching her cheeks, her nose, her eyes, and lingering for a moment on her forehead. Then he straightened. "Let's go see Doc."

She felt the red flooding her face. "Just a minute." She bent to retrieve his hat, conscious now of the people around them.

"Thank you." His tone was a soft caress. With his arm around her, they moved off toward the sign that indicated the doctor's office.

Abby tried to collect her thoughts. The feel of his body against her side was disconcerting. She was supremely conscious of this man, of his appeal to her. She had been feeling that appeal since the day of her arrival. And now he had kissed her!

She felt the heat suffusing her face. And she had let him. In fact, she had helped him. How could she have forgotten the lesson she had learned so painfully from Art? Men did not want a person, a partner. What they wanted was a possession, a pretty little thing who would echo their beliefs and be there all the time to do for them. She did not think she was a selfish woman, but she could not subjugate her life to a man. She had a career; she had worked hard to succeed in it. She did not intend to give it up.

By now they had entered the small room that

served as the doctor's office. Outside the crowd was breaking up, everyone returning to their private enjoyment of the town.

Dan took the wadded piece of cloth from his shoulder. "Thanks, Abby. You did a great job."

She pulled herself out of the circle of his arm, which he had not bothered to remove from around her waist. "You didn't tell me about the end of the skit."

"What end?" His attempted look of innocence didn't quite come off.

"You know exactly what I mean." She forced herself to use a cold tone.

"Aw, come on, Abby. Don't get mad." His grin was warm. "It was all part of the skit."

She said the first words that came to her mind. "You were planning to kiss Nan?"

His hesitation lasted several seconds too long. "Sure. Why not?"

Abby shook her head. She would certainly not tell him what she was feeling, especially that first stab of jealousy at the thought of him kissing Nan Sherwood. It had been jealousy, there was no doubt of that fact. It frightened her. She had no business having such strong feelings about Dan Jenkins. He was a stranger to her—and she meant for him to stay that way.

But even more frightening was the surge of elation she had felt at the realization that he was hedging, that he had not intended to kiss Nan at all.

"I think you took unfair advantage of me," she said crisply. "With the audience watching and all."

His hand closed around hers and he pulled her closer. "You're right," he admitted softly, his free hand reaching out to touch her cheek in a swift caress. "I didn't mean to kiss Nan. I didn't mean to kiss you either. It just happened."

She maintained a cold silence. If she opened her mouth it might curve into a smile like his.

He moved a step nearer. "You were there, so close to me. So beautiful." His voice sank to a hypnotic whisper. "I wanted to kiss you. So I did."

He traced the line of her chin with a warm fingertip. "I can't help it, Abby. You have that effect on me."

And you on me, she wanted to say. But she didn't. She just shook her head. "I still think you were wrong. I'll bring the dress back later."

He smiled, a lazy warm smile that threatened to melt her bones. "I'll come along and wait while you change."

"No!" She forced herself to glare at him, though she knew inwardly that a part of her wanted that very thing—wanted to invite Dan Jenkins into her trailer and let him do what his eyes so clearly indicated. But she had already decided against any involvement with the man.

"That won't be necessary." She kept her tone as chill as possible. "I can manage quite well myself."

"I'm sure you can." His smile faded and was replaced by an expression of serious concern. "I didn't mean to offend you."

This apology was too much for Abby. Or was it the fact that he had moved closer again? She turned and hurried toward the door. Her hand was on the knob when his voice halted her. "Abby?"

She spun on her heels. "What do you want?"

His eyes surveyed her gravely and then he nodded. "I see it now." He took a step toward her. "Tell me, Abby, why are you afraid of me?"

The question stopped her; her hand froze on the knob. It was another of those questions she couldn't answer truthfully. How could she admit that she was scared to death of him? That the pull between them was so strong that she hardly knew how to fight it?

"Don't be ridiculous," she snapped. Maybe if she were rude enough he would leave her alone. "Why should I be afraid of you?"

He shook his head slightly and his eyes darkened. "You tell me, Abby." He shrugged and spread his hands. "I've always thought I was a pretty nice guy. Never hurt a fly."

This reference to their former spider and fly word-play almost made her smile, but she managed to suppress it. "I told you, I'm not afraid of you."

"You don't dislike me, do you?" His forehead wrinkled in a frown. "I mean, I'm not the smartest man in the world but I never thought I was so dense that I'd believe a woman responds to me when she doesn't." His eyes fastened on hers. "You did respond to me, I know that."

She felt the scarlet flooding her cheeks, but she refused to lower her eyes. "You took me by surprise. I was into the role."

He did not reply to this and for a long moment they both stood silent. She wanted to lower her eyes, to look somewhere else. What she saw in his dark eyes was even more unsettling than desire. For she saw tenderness, concern, caring. For a breathless second she considered admitting the truth, throwing herself against him and blurting out all her fear and longing.

But then her common sense took over. Of course

men could be tender, concerned, caring—until a woman wanted a life and career of her own.

She took a step backward. "I have to go now. Goodbye, Dan." Using his name was a mistake. She knew that when her voice broke in the middle of the word, but she didn't wait to see how he would respond. She yanked open the door and practically fled into the street. Still, she was not quick enough to avoid hearing the soft laughter of the man she left behind.

4

~oooooooooooo~

The next morning Abby woke with a headache. She lay looking up at the low ceiling and tears welled up in her eyes. Why did life have to be so confusing?

Her stomach grumbled ominously, reminding her that she hadn't eaten for far too long. Yesterday's lunch had been her last solid meal. When she left Dan after the performance she had gone directly back to her trailer. Oblivious to the admiring glances of the spectators, letting the skirt of the red gown trail behind her unheeded in the dust, she had moved almost blindly through the crowd.

Once within the privacy of the trailer she had kicked off her shoes, stripped off the gown and black stockings, jerked the feather from her hair, and scrubbed the rouge and lipstick from her face. Then, once more wearing her regular clothes, she had returned to the kitchen table to make revisions on the draft of her article.

She had even succeeded in pushing Dan to the back of her mind. She could not get rid of him entirely, but she did succeed in attending to her work. So well did she succeed, in fact, that it was dark before she rose from the table. And then, feeling exhausted, she had showered and thrown herself into bed.

Another sigh welled up from deep within Abby. She might have known that it really wouldn't work. It had been hard enough to keep Dan out of her thoughts while she struggled with stubborn revisions. But with nothing else filling her mind, thoughts of him came racing back.

Even now she felt her body reacting to the memory of that kiss. Desire stirred deep within her and she groaned aloud. This whole thing was ridiculous. She had work to do; she couldn't afford to lie around mooning over a man. Nor could she afford the sleepless night she had just spent—a night of tossing and turning that had left her feeling miserable, and probably looking even worse.

With an exclamation of disgust she threw back the covers. Number one on her list of things to do was to catch the car into town. First, she had her revisions to mail. Then she would pick up a few supplies. That way she could cook some meals for herself and avoid going so often to the cantina. Avoid seeing Dan too, she told herself. The sensible thing to do was to finish her assignment as soon as possible and get out of here.

If it had been only the brochure, she would have been tempted to call the deal off. But a chance to write for *Vacation Today* couldn't be ignored. Her career was on the line, and an article for that magazine would do a lot to move it along. Only a crazy woman would walk out on a deal like that. And she wasn't crazy. Not yet, at least.

Abby forced herself to her feet and moved into the shower. That's it, she told herself, keep moving. Keep busy. That way there was not so much time to think.

She waited at the front gate, wearing a pair of beige slacks and a soft pink pullover, at a few minutes before ten. Jim Seccord, coming by, saw her and asked, "Going into town?"

Abby nodded and tapped the envelope under her arm. "I've got some revisions here that need to go out, and I want to pick up a few things."

"Not going to visit a casino? Who knows, you might strike it rich."

Abby shook her head. "Not me. I don't like gambling. I'm a very practical person."

The manager's eyes twinkled. "You don't believe in getting something for nothing, huh?"

Abby smiled. "That's about it."

"Well, enjoy the trip." He turned into the cantina.

Abby glanced down at her watch. The car should be coming any minute now. The sound of an approaching motor made her turn as a Mustang pulled up. "Going into town?" Dan Jenkins asked as cheerfully as though nothing had occurred between them.

Abby nodded briefly. "When the car comes."

Dan grinned. "The car is here. My turn to drive today."

For a moment she could not reply. The last thing she needed was a ride into town with this man. "Jim said there would be a company car. A station wagon."

Dan nodded. "There is, but it needs repairs. So I volunteered mine. Hop in."

She considered backing out—pleading a sudden headache, a stomachache, anything to keep from going with him. But the revisions did need to get mailed, and she had already admitted that she planned to go. To back out now would convince him he was right—that she was afraid of him.

"Sure." The word wasn't as enthusiastic as she would have liked it to be, but she climbed swiftly in, depositing the manuscript on the seat between them.

There was silence in the car as Dan pulled away. They were out on the main highway, moving toward Vegas before he spoke. Abby had kept her eyes resolutely on the scenery, so the sound of his voice half startled her.

"Abby, I'm sorry about yesterday."

The words surprised her almost as much as the tone of apology, and she turned to look at him.

"I really am. It was a damn fool thing to do, taking you by surprise like that. I did take advantage."

She didn't quite know how to respond to this. It was all so unexpected.

"I know I embarrassed you," he continued. "I know you had no idea it was coming. Truthfully, neither did I. As I told you last night, I just got carried away by the moment."

He smiled, his teeth gleaming white beneath the

curving handlebar moustache. "But now that I'm being so truthful, I have to admit something else."

"What?" She couldn't stop herself from asking.

"I've been wanting to kiss you for a long time. Since just about the first time I saw you, when you were stepping off the bus."

"You saw me then?"

Dan nodded. "And wanted to kiss you."

His grin was broad but she did not return it. "I haven't time for romance," she replied stiffly. "I have a career to think of."

"Some people have combined both," he observed dryly.

Abby shook her head. "Some men," she replied.

Dan gave her a long look. "Some women too," he said finally.

Abby shook her head. "I've heard that. But I don't believe it's true. It didn't work for my mother. Marriage ruined her career as an artist. It didn't work for me, either. I'm not going to fall into that trap again."

Dan ran a hand through his hair and whistled softly. "I didn't think I'd proposed," he said dryly. "This isn't the nineteenth century, you know, when a single kiss was sufficient to compromise a woman."

Embarrassment flooded over Abby. He was making her sound silly. "I suppose I was overreacting," she admitted. "But I don't even want kissing."

The Mustang purred down the highway, and Dan cleared his throat. "At the risk of offending you again, which I really don't want to do, Abby, I have to reply to that. I know it's not polite to contradict a

lady. But in this case . . . I have to say that the way
you returned my kiss indicated that you very much
wanted kissing.''

She did not know how to refute this and so
continued her silence, her gaze on the desert
outside the car windows.

"This is the twentieth century, Abby. You've
been living in the past in more ways than one."

She did not look at him, but she heard every
word distinctly.

"If a woman's not interested in marriage, if she
wants to put her career first, that's still no reason
she should close herself off from men and their
companionship. If you want to be a good writer,
you have to have experience. You have to live.
Fortunately, you can do that these days. No one's
interested in policing your morals. No one cares."

She looked at him then—at the broad shoulders
stretching his plaid shirt, at the powerful thighs
beneath his blue jeans, at the strong brown hands
gripping the wheel—and she realized that this was
the first time she had seen him in ordinary clothes.
But clothes didn't make the man—not in this case.
Not for her. No matter what he was wearing Dan
Jenkins was an attractive man, a man to catch a
woman's eye.

"Give it some thought," Dan suggested and
concentrated again on his driving.

Returning her gaze to the desert outside her
window, Abby did just that. Here was a person to
whom she was strongly attracted. How would a
man behave in a similar situation? A man who put
his career first, who didn't want any serious entan-
glements? The answer seemed clear. He would

pursue a short, no-strings relationship. That's what men had been doing for years, hadn't they?

Life had been very lonely this last year. She had to admit that. Her marriage had made her accustomed to some kind of male companionship. Why not enjoy herself on this short assignment? Men did it all the time. And seeing Dan would enrich her life, her experience.

"Love doesn't have to be forever," he said softly, his eyes leaving the road to linger momentarily on her face.

"It seldom is," she replied, her voice revealing more pain than she had meant it to.

"I don't mean like that," he said. "I mean, love can be for a moment's time. People can 'choose,' beforehand, to make love a short-term thing, to give it boundaries."

Abby shook her head. "I don't want anything to do with love," she said stubbornly. "That's out of my life for good."

Dan nodded. "I hear you." One hand moved from the steering wheel to pat hers briefly. "But will you consider a 'close' friendship?"

Abby couldn't help smiling. He really was fun to be with. "I might consider it," she said slowly, relishing the feel of his fingers on hers.

"Good." He left the subject as his hand left hers, and he began a running commentary on the area they were driving through. Time passed quickly and Abby was surprised when they reached the post office parking lot.

"I'll only be a minute," she said.

Dan nodded. "No hurry. We've got plenty of time. It's my day off."

Abby digested this as she went through the now familiar motions of mailing a manuscript. So this was his day off and he had come into town. Back at the car she said what was on her mind. "I'm sure you have plans for today, Dan. Just leave me off somewhere and tell me where and when you want to pick me up." A man this attractive must have a woman somewhere, she told herself.

"Are you planning to meet someone?" he asked.

The question took her so by surprise that she blurted out "No, of course not" without thinking.

His smile showed great satisfaction. "Neither am I. We might as well stay together. Where did you want to go next?"

"I need a few groceries so I can have a meal in the trailer now and then. Do you know a good place?"

"Sure do. I'll take you there."

After shopping, they loaded three bags of groceries into the back seat of the Mustang. Then Abby collapsed in the front seat with a sigh. She was still not completely acclimated to the heat. After all, Pittsburgh had been ankle deep in snow when she left it less than a week before.

"Tired?" Dan asked when he climbed in the driver's side and shut the door.

"A little. The weather's so warm."

Dan nodded. "One of our main attractions." He swung the car out of the parking lot.

Soon they were driving down the strip, past the glittering casinos, the shining, nighttime fairy-tale town that in the daylight only looked sad and gaudy to her.

"Do you want to stop anywhere?" Dan asked.

"What for?"

He laughed. "People have been known to gamble here. Thought you might like to give it a try."

Abby shook her head. "Not me. I've never believed in that kind of thing."

Dan smiled. "Gambling is a science. There are ways of winning."

Abby's retort was fast and sharp. "Not for me. I intend to keep my money. I work hard for it."

Was he a gambler? she wondered. Did he like that kind of excitement and risk?

"Where were you born?" he asked, his hand covering hers, and the contact drove all thought of casinos out of her mind.

"Pittsburgh," she replied. "On Kentucky Avenue. That is, I lived there. In a big frame house." Her face grew wistful. "I loved it there. The huge old trees lining the street. They were like friends."

"Don't you ever go back?"

She shook her head. "I haven't for a while. Mom and Dad sold the house. It's not the same with someone else living in it." She smiled. "It was a happy house. That's the way I want to remember it."

Dan nodded. "Sometimes memories are best. Things never look the same years later. You can't go home again, as a famous novelist once observed. So when did you decide to be a writer?"

Abby's chuckle was warm. "Probably when I was two or three. I don't really remember. It seems to me that I've always been writing. I love it."

Dan nodded. "You're one of the fortunate ones, having a job you really enjoy."

Abby nodded. "I know. But what . . ."

"I suppose you were smart in school."

"Of course," Abby replied, laughing. "And I was editor of the school paper. I studied journalism at the University of Pennsylvania. After that I worked for a magazine for a while. But then I got married and started freelancing."

"How long . . ." Dan began.

"Five years," she replied grimly. "And then I got divorced. And I don't want to talk about that."

He nodded sympathetically. "Of course."

The conversation continued. He was so skillful at drawing her out that it wasn't until they pulled into the lane leading to Old Vegas that she realized she knew no more about him than she had before. He had gotten practically her entire life story without divulging anything about himself.

"Hey, I've been doing all the talking," she said. "Tell me something about yourself."

A closed look came over his face as he smiled. "Nothing much to tell."

"Where are you from?"

"Anyplace and everyplace," he replied. "I like to move around. But look, here we are, back at the old homestead. I'll drive around by your trailer, and help you unload the stuff."

Abby nodded. "Thanks. I can give you back the dress then."

Dan shook his head. "I want you to keep it. It's your gown, Abby. No one else should wear it."

The car bumped to a stop. "But you need it for the shop," she protested. "And the skit."

"Don't worry about it. Nan's backed out of the skit. Says she can't handle it." Fingers on the door handle, he grinned at her. "Don't suppose it was the prospect of kissing me that put her off, do you?"

Luckily, there was no need to answer this for he

was already climbing out of the car and reaching for her grocery bags.

He helped her carry them in, setting them on the kitchen counter. "How're you making out?" he asked, glancing around the trailer.

"OK." She managed a shaky smile. Here in the confines of the trailer her sense of his physical presence was almost overwhelming. Every breath she took seemed filled with the male scent of him, and her fingers longed to reach out and touch him. If he took her in his arms now . . .

She was being extremely foolish, she told herself. Just because he was a good talker—had shown her a possible way out of her dilemma—didn't mean she should fall immediately into his arms.

"Well . . ." He seemed to have become embarrassed. "Guess I better go. Got some letters to write today."

Abby nodded. She was suddenly conscious that she didn't want him to leave, that she would miss his presence. But she also knew that she had to have time—time to think about this new kind of "love" he had told her about. Time to decide whether he was right about it. She looked at him uncertainly. "Yes. I've got work to do too."

He moved toward her, across the tiny kitchen, and her heart jumped up into her throat. But he stepped silently by her, turning only when he reached the door. "See you later, Abby. You will consider what I said?"

She nodded. "Yes, Dan, I will."

"Good. Bye then."

He closed the door carefully after himself and the breath left Abby's lungs in a great whoosh. The trailer seemed suddenly to have grown much larger without him in it, she thought, as she began to take the groceries out of the bags and put them away.

A faint scent of his aftershave lingered in the air and she smiled slightly. It had truly been a pleasant morning; she had enjoyed talking about herself. A frown creased her forehead then and she paused, the refrigerator door open, a carton of milk in her hand. She had told him plenty about herself and learned very little about him.

What kind of man was he really? Where had he come from? Was he a drifter of some kind?

She put the milk on the shelf and shut the door. He'd said he liked to move around. A sudden picture of the Strip flashed into her mind. What had he said about gambling? That it was a science? That a person could win?

She shook her head. She had never thought of herself as a particularly puritanical person, but she definitely disapproved of gambling. She was aware, certainly, that many people found gambling amusing, a form of recreation for which they paid as they would have paid for any other kind of fun. But she couldn't see it that way.

What about Dan? she wondered. How did he view gambling? Did he really think of it as a science? Did he gamble himself? Was that the reason he was here in Old Vegas, working in a dead-end job? Had he gambled away everything he had and started working there to get a stake to start over?

There was no way to know, of course. It was not the sort of thing one asked a man about. But Dan must be at least thirty. He was well-educated and articulate. And something told her that he had once had money—a lot of it.

Abby shrugged. None of that mattered. She was contemplating a short-term relationship. One month. Two at the most. Then it would be over. It really didn't make any difference about Dan's background. Maybe his being a drifter made it even better. He wouldn't be expecting permanence. Yes, maybe that was the way to go. Women were liberated now—they could do everything men could do. Men, of course, had been doing this kind of thing for years, though sometimes without telling their partners until it was too late.

That couldn't happen with Dan, though. She would be up front with him. She already was. And he could hardly object to the kind of relationship that he had spelled out for her himself.

The last of the groceries were put away and Abby decided to open a can of soup. Yes, indeed, she had to admit that Dan's suggestion needed thinking about, a lot of thinking about. And the more she thought the closer she came to seeing the practicality of the whole thing. She threw a glance at the framed sepia photo of herself in the red dress. Yes, she was going to do a lot of thinking.

5

~eeeeeeeeee~

Abby spent the next morning and afternoon thinking. She examined Dan's proposition many times. Every minute that she wasn't actually working on the article or the brochure he was in her mind.

She thought of him in the late morning as she crossed the square toward the cantina. She wanted to see Jim Seccord before she did any more writing.

He answered her tap with a brisk "Come in."

She pushed open the door.

"Hello, Abby. Sit down. What can I do for you?"

"Nothing much. Just wanted to ask if you have any suggestions," she said as she settled into a chair. "Anything you want me to add." She gave him a quick rundown of what she had done so far. "I plan to add several photos of the dramatizations," she went on. "I think they add a real interest."

The manager nodded. "Yes, a lot of people have come back just to see them all. Speaking of which . . ." His eyes went to her face. "Let me congratulate you on your performance the other day."

She felt the blush coming but determined to ignore it. "I'm afraid I'm not much of an actress." Her laugh betrayed her nervousness. "That was my first public performance."

The manager's smile was cherubic. "And not your last. In fact, it was so successful that I want to ask you to continue in the part."

All the breath seemed to leave Abby's body and she sat paralyzed, her mouth suddenly as dry as the desert outside. Finally she found some words. "You must be kidding."

He shook his head. "Not at all. It was very successful. We want to repeat it at least once a day."

"But not with me." Even as she said it she felt a wave of regret so strong that she almost recalled them. "If Nan doesn't want to do it, one of the other young women will."

The manager shook his head. "No such luck," he said. "It seems that none of them are aspiring actresses. They've all turned down the part."

"All?" Abby was aware that she was echoing him stupidly, but she found it very difficult to believe that none of those women wanted to play the role. Wanted, she corrected herself truthfully, to be kissed by Dan. "I-I don't know what to say."

"Say yes," Jim Seccord suggested cheerfully. "You can keep the gown." An almost devilish grin gave his face an impish look. "And think of the invaluable experience you'll be getting."

Laughter burst from Abby. She couldn't help it. He was turning her own words back on her—and effectively too. "All right, Jim," she conceded. "I guess I'll have to give in. I'm more or less hoist on my own petard."

The manager's eyes twinkled. "There's one more thing you can do for me."

Abby laughed. "From the look in your eyes I'm not sure I should say yes."

Seccord's laughter was high-pitched and merry. "You're getting too suspicious. All I want to know is—what the devil is a petard?"

This time Abby's laughter was louder. "It means blown up by your own bomb," she explained. "A petard was a case for explosives."

The manager grinned. "Thank you. I'll make that my new word for the day."

"I don't think it's going to be a very useful addition to your vocabulary," she couldn't resist saying.

Seccord shrugged. "A man never knows when a piece of information will be useful."

Since Abby's recent declaration of the same was still quite clear in her mind—and apparently in his—she could hardly refute this. "Of course," she said, deciding to accept this gentle raillery in kind. "My thought exactly."

Seccord broke into laughter then too.

Getting to her feet, Abby said, "This is a fun job, Jim. I'll be sorry to leave it."

"It's too soon to be talking of leaving," he replied. "You need a few more weeks to get all the information."

"We'll see."

"At any rate, thanks again for playing Lizzie, or

Abby, as her name is now. We've decided to do the skit once a day. Around two. Can you start today?"

Abby nodded. "I'll be there."

"Great."

Seccord turned back to his desk and Abby made her way outside, her mind a jumble of emotions. Why had none of the women wanted to do this? Several of them were quite attractive.

But that question soon faded from her mind. A quick glance at her watch told her that it was now almost eleven. She'd better get back to the trailer and check on the dress. And the black stockings. Where had she put those stockings?

The next hour passed quickly as Abby laid out each item she was to wear and examined it. But by twelve there was nothing more to do. She considered having some lunch, but a convention of butterflies seemed to have taken over in her stomach and she was afraid the addition of food would only add to the chaos.

The hands of her watch moved pitifully slow, but they did move and eventually it was time to get dressed. She surveyed herself in the mirror. Her lips and cheeks were bright with rouge and she stuck the red feather at a sharp angle into the heavy black coil of her hair. Yes, she supposed she looked the part. The petticoat had another rip started in it. She had checked that. She was ready, she told herself, as she turned away and went down the trailer's steps into the sun.

She tried to concentrate on the beauty of the day, on the spurts of sandy dust raised by her shoes, on anything but the fact that soon she would be running to Dan's side and he would be kissing her.

She wanted that kiss; she knew it with absolute certainty. But she did not let herself think any further. There would be time enough later to consider what Dan had said to her, to decide if she wanted to try this new kind of relationship he had spoken so well of.

She entered the coolness of the Arizona Club just as the sheriff's voice came booming over the loudspeaker, inviting the visitors to gather in the square to witness some of Black Bart's shenanigans. Her hands smoothed nervously at the sides of her gown and she leaned a trembling elbow on the high counter.

"Don't know how you can do it," a soft voice declared.

Abby turned to meet Nan Sherwood's smile.

"It nearly scared me to death."

Abby managed a timid smile. "I'm not exactly calm and collected," she revealed.

Nan shook her blonde curls. "Nobody can tell it by looking at you."

"Thanks." Abby turned back toward the door. She couldn't say exactly how she felt. When she considered all the people watching her, she was aware of some nervousness about her performance. But that was overshadowed by what was coming, by the fact that in a few minutes Dan Jenkins was going to kiss her.

As she moved toward the window to get a better view, she saw Dan leave Hard Rock Pete's. He was in his shirt sleeves this time. Abby wondered absently if the "stain" had refused to come out of his coat. Anyway, it would show better on the shirt. She licked her lips nervously. He was nearing the railroad car now, moving confidently, a man sure of his own worth.

Her mouth curved in an unconscious smile. He was really a terrific-looking man. An awful lot of fun to be with. What would it be like if she took him up on his offer? If she allowed herself this "limited-time" relationship?

He had said it could be very good, that people could be caring even while they had a time limit to their "love." She understood the idea; she could grasp it intellectually. But emotionally it was quite foreign to her. "Love," as she had always thought of it, had no boundaries, no limits, whether of time or of anything else.

"Hey, gambling man!" Black Bart stepped from behind the railroad car and dropped his horse's reins. He wore the black clothes that his name implied and his guns hung low on his hips.

Dan turned slowly. "Are you talking to me?"

Abby's smile grew. She liked the idea of not having any special, set lines. It was more fun this way. It gave them more room to move around.

"Yeah, fancy man. I'm talking to you." Bart's sneer was perfection itself.

"Well, what do you want?"

Dan faced the gunfighter with confidence and Abby had a sudden strong sense of reality. This might all be for show—a little make-believe to entertain the patrons—but Dan's confidence and strength was very real. She felt somehow that if this really had been the "old" days, and Black Bart and his six-shooter had been real, Dan would still have been as confident and manly.

"I want my money back," Bart growled, and his hands dropped to his hips, to the six-shooter hanging there. "You cheated me."

Dan's voice was steely; little shivers tingled down Abby's spine. "You're mistaken, my friend. Dapper Dan never cheats. He doesn't need to."

Abby's eyes left Dan for a moment to appraise the watching crowd. They were all engrossed in the little melodrama unfolding before them. Even the children stood silent, their eyes wide as they watched.

"I said you cheated me. I want my money back or else." Bart's threat quivered in the air.

For a long minute Dan faced him, contempt on his face. Then he shook his head. "If you can't take your losses like a man, it's best not to gamble. Remember that." He turned and began to walk toward the saloon. Behind him, Bart's gun left his holster and the shot rang out.

This time Dan hit the ground more quickly and the hand that clutched his shoulder fell away almost at once. Yes, Abby thought, the white shirt made the "stain" much more effective.

Bart was already on his horse as she hurried out the door, skirt held high. "Dan!" This time she knew she was acting; this time she didn't have the terrible feeling that the whole thing was real.

He remained lying on the ground until she reached him. By then the sound of Bart's horse had faded.

"Dan! You're hit! You're bleeding!" Abby had had no intention of expanding her part. She didn't know where the words came from.

"I'm all right, Abby." He pushed himself to a

sitting position, being careful not to use his "injured" arm. "He just winged me."

"You shouldn't play with men like him." With a sense of amazement Abby realized that she was deliberately building her part.

"Hey, sweetheart. Gambling is my business. I can't be too choosy or I won't have any game at all."

"I don't like it." She realized that the vehemence in her tone was real. "It's too dangerous. Look at you now." She sent him a disgusted look before she turned to rip a piece off the petticoat.

Holding the wadded material against the stain, Dan allowed her to help him to his feet. "That's a girl," he said, throwing an arm around her shoulder. "Just help me along to Doc's."

"I ought to leave you here," she ad-libbed. "You're nothing but trouble."

Dan's eyes twinkled. He was enjoying this immensely. "Come on now, sweetheart. You're my girl and you know it."

"And you're a conceited—" The sentence went unfinished as Dan swung her around and bent to take her lips. This kiss was not so brief as the first had been. This kiss was slow and easy. His lips possessed hers, teasing, caressing, persuading, demanding—until she lost all thought of his "wounded" arm. So far removed was she from the reality of the situation that when the crowd began to applaud she was startled and almost jumped.

Dan's hands steadied her. "Easy, Abby," he whispered. "They like us. We're a success."

A nod was all she could manage as she turned and began to walk him toward the doctor's office. He stopped outside the door to pull her even closer. "Have you thought about what I said?" he asked, his lips against her ear.

"Yes." The word was a mere whisper, but he heard it and his grip on her waist tightened.

"Good. Will you have dinner with me tonight? To celebrate our success." He felt the momentary stiffening of her body. "No strings attached, Abby. Just a pleasant evening. You call the shots. OK?"

This time she felt the tensing of his muscles. Was he preparing himself for rejection again? She hesitated only for a moment. "OK, Dan."

She heard the long drawn-out sigh. "Thank you, Abby. Around seven?"

She turned to face him, easing herself out of the circle of his arm with a reluctance she hoped didn't show on her face. "Yes, that sounds good."

His smile appeared. "Shall we make a real celebration of it? Get kind of dressed up? I do have a regular suit."

She nodded. "Yes, I'd like that."

He bent to drop a kiss on her forehead. "See you then."

At six P.M. Abby surveyed the contents of her closet and wrinkled her nose in exasperation. She hadn't brought much with her; she certainly hadn't expected to need any fancy dresses. But this was going to be a special evening. At least it could be—from the look in Dan's eyes. She did have a pair of high heels and one good dress, though she wasn't sure what had prompted her to include it in her packing. Probably the fact that it took so little room and could literally be crumpled into a ball without wrinkling, she thought with a smile, pulling it from the closet.

71

She felt like wearing something new tonight, something to signify a beginning, but this dress would do. Its pale green deepened the green of her eyes, or so she had been told. She laid the dress carefully across the bed and went to the small dresser for her lacy underwear.

The trailer was small, but its bathroom did have a tub. Abby pinned her hair high on her head, poured in sweet-smelling bathsalts and filled the tub. Then she climbed in, luxuriating in the bubbles and the scent.

It was fun getting ready for a special evening out, she thought, as she lifted a slim leg from the bubbles and examined it thoughtfully. This was a part of life she'd been missing by closing herself off as she had, refusing to go out with anyone.

She leaned back in the bubbles. It was time she recognized one thing. Whether she decided to take Dan up on his offer or not, she was enjoying knowing him. She felt more alive, more enthusiastic about life than she had for a long, long time. And that was due to her knowing Dan Jenkins. She was very clear on that.

Pushing a frothy mass of bubbles idly back and forth across the water, Abby wondered for the hundredth time why a man like Dan Jenkins was wasting his life. He was so dynamic, so forceful. What kind of a career had he abandoned to come to this make-believe town and lead a make-believe life? Maybe tonight she would find out.

She dried herself slowly, conscious of a new awareness of her body. It was a good body. Men had called it beautiful—men beside Art. But she had not been paying much attention to it since the divorce, more or less taking it for granted.

That was ended now, she thought, as she gazed down at the soft roundness of her breasts, the flat plane of her stomach. How would Dan like her body? Would he find it beautiful, desirable?

He had found her so before, she thought, slipping into her underwear and adjusting the lacy bra. She had seen that in his eyes. She pulled on her pantyhose and half-slip and returned to the mirror to do her face.

Her makeup was much more subdued now. Subtle, understated—not the garish brightness that marked Abby the saloon girl. She applied eye shadow, green again to pick up the color of her eyes, a pale coral lipstick to outline her mouth and then she was ready to do her hair. She brushed its black glossiness vigorously, a soft smile on her lips. Should she let it hang free or should she pin it up? How would Dan like it best?

She decided to put the dress on first. Pulling it from the hanger, she slipped it gently over her head. It slid down, its silkiness satisfying against her bare skin. She pulled up the side zipper and adjusted the draped, crossed bodice over her breasts. No cleavage here, she thought. At least, not as much as the red velvet dress displayed. She glanced affectionately toward the closet where it hung, waiting for tomorrow's performance. She pulled the full sleeves of the green dress down to her wrists and adjusted her watch, then tied the matching sash around her narrow waist. A quick twirl assured her that the skirt hung properly.

This had always been one of her favorite dresses, she thought, picking up the hairbrush again. Perhaps due to its shade of green or its durability. She didn't know. At any rate, she was glad she'd thrown it in. Tonight was definitely a night for dressing up, a special night. She grabbed up a handful of hairpins. A special night called for a special hairdo.

At five minutes to seven she nodded with satisfaction. Her hair was massed in three dark coils, one on top of her head and one to each side. Yes, that was just right. Digging in her traveling jewel case, she pulled out the dangling earrings that had been a gift from her grandmother. The emeralds in them were real and they were very old. It was for that reason that she carried them with her everywhere. Better to wear them than to leave them at home and risk their being stolen. She fastened them in her ears and reached for her perfume. Just as she touched the nozzle, a rap sounded on the door. "Coming."

She smiled as she opened the door. She really couldn't help herself.

"Wow! What else can I say?" Dan shrugged eloquently, raising the shoulders in his beige suit.

Abby let her eyes travel slowly over him. His suit jacket clung to his broad shoulders, its light color contrasting nicely with his dark skin and hair. He wore a white shirt and a dark brown tie. "Wow, yourself," Abby said with a smile. "I like that even better than your Dapper Dan outfit."

He grinned. "Thank you." He eyed her speculatively. "Hmmm."

"What is that supposed to mean?" Abby felt the laughter welling up from within her.

"I don't know whether I prefer this dress or the red one." His smile was a caress; she was warmed by it. "This one shows me a different side of you," he continued. "Refined, ladylike, cool." He reached out to take her hand. She felt his warm fingers curling around hers. "I like this one. But I like the red one too. That one shows a fiery, vibrant part of you."

The laughter bubbled out of her, and she stepped down toward him. "How many sides to me do you suppose there are?"

His arm went around her waist. "I don't know, Abby. But I'd like the chance to see them all."

6

When Dan helped her out of the Mustang half an hour later, Abby was surprised to find that their destination was a small, subdued restaurant away from the glitter and glamor of the Vegas Strip.

"I hope you don't mind," he said, his hand enclosing hers. "We can go somewhere else if you'd rather. I just thought . . . I got the idea that you aren't too fond of casinos. And this place has great food. What do you think?"

"I think I like your choice of restaurants. But I warn you, I'm starving."

He pulled her close to his side. "Me too. All that melodrama must have given us huge appetites. I think you'll like this place. They've got a great chef."

They were met inside the door by a smiling headwaiter. "Good evening, sir. Right this way."

The table was a good one, Abby noted, and she

liked the atmosphere of the place. It was small and rather homey and the smell of delicious food hung in the air. She sniffed appreciatively. "Hmmm, smells good."

Dan grinned as he pulled out her chair. "Tastes good too."

After some consultation over the menu, they decided on the beef stroganoff. The salad came, with a sweet-and-sour house dressing that Abby wished she could get the recipe for. But when she asked, the waitress replied that it was a secret. "The chef won't give it to anyone," she confided with a smile.

The beef stroganoff was superb, but Abby's attention was no longer on the food. Their table was very small; under it, Dan's knees pressed against hers. She felt the roughness of his trousers, his warmth, and her own body began to grow warm. So far he hadn't mentioned their relationship. Not with words, at least, but his eyes were very eloquent. Dark and warm, they seemed to be holding an invitation, an invitation that she wanted more and more to accept.

The meal finished, they sipped their coffee. "The food was delicious," Abby said. "This is a fine place."

"I discovered it accidentally," Dan said. "But we've talked enough about the place and the food. Now it's time to talk about us."

Abby's fingers tightened on the coffee cup, but she remained silent.

He reached across the table to cover her free hand with his. "What about it, Abby? Have you been thinking about what I said?"

She swallowed over the lump in her throat.

77

"How could I help it?" she replied. "I see you all the time. And in the skit . . ."

His eyes grew warmer and his knee pressed harder against hers. "And what kind of conclusion have you come to?" he asked softly, opening her hand and tracing the lines of her palm with a gentle finger.

Abby stared at their hands. It was almost as though he were touching some other part of her. A delicious little shiver quivered down her spine and she wanted very much to get up from the table and walk into his waiting arms.

The game was fun, she realized, and for that reason she would like to prolong it. But beyond that was a nagging little fear. It had been so long since she'd been with a man. What if it didn't go well?

"I haven't come to a conclusion yet," she said finally. "But I'm willing to talk about it some more." She summoned a shaky smile. "The whole idea is very new to me. Oh, I've heard about relationships like that. About 'open marriages' and people just living together." A flush spread across her cheeks. "And other things too, but I never thought of doing them myself."

Dan's smile was gentle. "I can imagine. But it isn't that far out. Not now. The world's changing, you know. People's values are changing."

Abby frowned. "I thought some values never changed."

Dan's dark face grew serious. "Everything changes, Abby. That's what life's all about. Change. Nothing stays the same. If you try to make it stay, try to keep it, you'll just be disappointed. Better to recognize that change is inevitable—and design your life accordingly."

Abby sighed. "But don't we all want to be safe? To know that we'll be loved forever?"

Dan patted the hand he held. "Of course we do, Abby. We want it so much that we fool ourselves into thinking we can get it."

"But people do love each other," she replied. "Some of them for a lifetime."

Dan nodded. "Sure, but have you ever wondered how they managed it?"

Abby shook her head. "No, not really."

"I think," said Dan, slowly lacing his fingers with hers, "I believe it's because of their awareness. They know about change, so they expect it. They expect to grow and change together."

Abby digested this.

"They don't expect to be safe and sure." He touched her cheek with strong gentle fingers in a swift tender caress. "Safety and security," he added, "don't come from other people, Abby. A liberated woman like you should know that. Those qualities come from within. You have to have them within yourself."

Abby nodded. "Yes, I know that. But then why do people need each other at all?"

Dan smiled. "You're leading me on, Abby. You know why. We all need companionship. It's from being involved with others that we learn some of the most important things about ourselves. We need each other in order to learn."

"But what . . ." The idea itself was fascinating to her. It almost made her forget the warm pressure of his fingers on hers. Almost. "What could we learn from each other?"

His smile was an intimate caress warming her whole body. "We won't know that till we try it. Life may be like a schoolroom, Abby, but unfortunately —or maybe fortunately—how can we be sure? The courses aren't always labeled. But every experience can teach us something about ourselves, about others. If we're willing to learn."

She put her free hand around the fingers that held hers. "Yes, Dan," she whispered. "I want to learn."

For a long moment he was silent, his eyes locked with hers. "Thank you, Abby," he breathed softly. "Thank you so much."

She saw his hesitation and realized that he was still fearful of offending her. "Do you want some dessert?" he asked, obviously unsure what to do next.

"No, thank you, Dan." Abby smiled slightly. "But I would like to know what you think our 'friendship' should be like."

The hand that clasped hers tightened and he grinned suddenly. "If we weren't sitting in this restaurant, I'd show you, Abby Holland. In fact, since we're through eating, you just come with me."

"Yes sir." Abby felt lightheaded. This was fun. Dan was fun. Why worry about anything?

He took care of the check, then guided her out the door. The stars burned brightly in the clear night sky. His arm under her elbow, he led her toward the car, but at her door he stopped. She turned to face him.

"Abby, oh Abby." His hands came up to frame her face, his palms warm against her cheeks, while his dark eyes searched hers. Then he pulled her close, his arms enveloping her. She was conscious of the warmth of his chest beneath her hands, his chin against her cheek, the curling ends of his moustache brushing her skin. Strange, she had not felt the moustache during their kiss that afternoon.

He pulled her slowly against his chest, his palms warm on her back. She luxuriated in the masculine feel of him, in the male scent of him. Then he was bending his head, his lips moving softly across her cheek. "Abby, Abby," he whispered softly. "You know what I want. Do you want it too?"

She did not hesitate. "Yes, Dan. Please, find us a place."

He did not kiss her then as she had expected he might, but swept her off her feet in a great bear hug and whirled her exuberantly through the air.

Fifteen minutes later he opened the door of a room and stepped aside for her to enter. "I'm sorry to bring you to the Strip," he said. "I know you don't like it. But these are the only kind of places in town."

She entered the room and turned to him. "It's all right, Dan. Come in and shut the door. Please."

He did just that, giving her that slow sweet smile as he crossed the room toward her. Then his arms went around her, drawing her to him, and his mouth found hers. This kiss was like none she had ever experienced. All evening she'd been waiting, waiting for the touch of him, the feel of his mouth so briefly known before.

Now, while his lips touched hers, every nerve cell in her body went into a kind of joyous clamor. This was wonderful, this was special. Her heightened senses sang the message. She gave herself to him fully, savoring his kiss and all it implied. There was no need to draw back, she told herself, no need to be afraid. She had made her decision. And she was glad.

When his mouth left hers, he held her off a little. "You're beautiful, Abby. The most beautiful woman I've ever seen."

She stood silently while he began to remove her clothes. His hands went to the coils of her upswept hair. Carefully they searched out the pins that held it, carefully they withdrew them. Her hair fell, a heavy sable cloud against her shoulders.

First he knelt at her feet, carefully taking off her pumps. Looking down at his dark head, she felt a great surge of tenderness. Then he rose, his hand seeking the zipper of her dress. He pulled it down, easing the dress gently from her shoulders and slowly down around her hips, Steadying herself with one hand on his broad shoulders, she stepped out of it and watched him lay it carefully on the second bed.

His eyes went to her breasts, then to the filmy bit of blue lace and nylon that covered them. She felt a flush of warmth creep up her body. His eyes were so frankly appreciative, so adoring. He bent to kiss a bare shoulder; she felt his moustache brush her throat. His head moved lower, seeking the whiteness of her breasts visible above the pale blue bra.

She felt the tingling of desire, the swelling of her breasts, and she knew that when the bra fell away, twin rosy peaks would be exposed, erect. Deep within her she was aware of a terrible yearning. She wanted this man, wanted to belong to him fully.

His hands moved over her back, seeking the fastener on her bra, while his lips remained caressing her shoulder and throat. Abby shivered—not from cold but from excitement. In his hands, warm and gentle, the fastener parted easily, and her bra joined the dress on the bed.

For a moment she felt the roughness of his jacket against her flesh and then he pulled back, his hands molding and lifting her breasts.

"So beautiful, Abby," he breathed, his voice husky with desire. He left a kiss on each rosy peak as his hands slid down over her ribcage to the circle of elastic that ringed her waist. Carefully he hooked his fingers inside that elastic, and with one smooth, graceful movement pulled her slip, pantyhose and panties down to her feet.

She stepped out of them, supposing he would rise, but for a moment he knelt there, his head bowed. Then, just as she was about to ask him what was wrong, she felt his lips on her instep. The sensation was like nothing she had ever felt before.

"Dan."

He paid no heed to her whispered calling of his name, and his mouth moved up her leg to her knee, her thigh, her flat stomach, up her ribcage again to her quivering breasts. Then he was pulling her into his arms, his hands spreading out, one on her back pressing her ever closer, the other cupping her bare bottom.

She felt the texture of his suit against bare skin, the pressure of his belt buckle against her flesh. She smelled the good male scent of him: the tanginess with a hint of sage that was his cologne and that something indefinable that was Dan's own scent. A deep sigh welled up from deep inside her. It was good to be held like this. Very, very good.

She had kept herself isolated for far too long, kept herself from enjoying what every human being needed. But no longer. Things would not be like that any longer. She was going to begin living again—and for that she had Dan to thank.

He pulled back the covers on the nearest bed and gently sat her down. "I'll be with you in a minute," he said softly. "Don't go away."

Her chuckle was equally soft. She had no intention of moving. Her body was glued to the spot just as her eyes were glued to him. Some part of her said it was immodest and unladylike to watch him disrobe, but that seemed pretty ridiculous under the circumstances. At any rate, she couldn't help herself.

She watched spellbound while he removed his coat and tie, putting them neatly beside her things. His shirt came next, revealing a mat of darkly curling hair that covered his chest and moved in a narrowing line down over his flat stomach to his belt buckle.

Fascinated, she watched his strong brown hands undo that buckle. His trousers slid to the floor, revealing pale orange jockey shorts molding his manhood. He sank to the side of the bed and slipped out of his shoes and socks. Then his shorts joined his suit and he was naked before her.

Without even thinking, Abby opened her arms to him. Then he was there beside her on the bed, his arms closing around her, and she pressed her soft body against his hard one. His hands pulled her close, eager hands clasping her to him. Her breath grew short as his mouth covered hers. Her breasts were pressed against his chest; she felt the wiry texture of his hair like a separate caress.

They lay on their sides, their bodies close against each other, Abby's arms around his neck, her hands clasped behind it. "God." His breath was warm against her ear. "How I want you!"

The words were music to her. She felt no hesitation. She meant to enjoy this evening.

His lips were tender and gentle, then teasing and withdrawing, leaving hers reaching toward them. Then suddenly they were back, possessive, demanding, and her own softened and opened to them. His tongue slipped softly into her mouth and hers went to meet it, touching and withdrawing, teasing his as he had teased her lips.

Suddenly he rolled over, his lean, athlete's body covering her, his mouth hard on hers. She could not tease him now, could not withdraw from his possessive kiss. Nor did she want to.

She felt the wonderful pressure of his body on hers, his chest against her sensitive breasts, his muscular legs entwined with hers, his rising manhood. It was strange, Abby thought. She was excited, aroused, wanting fulfillment, yet she felt a kind of warm, sweet lethargy creeping over her. She didn't want to rush anything.

Deep within her was the knowledge that this was going to be one of the best nights in her life. She was going to enjoy it to the fullest. As men did— and women too, if they believed in this new philosophy that Dan had explained to her. All this raced through her mind in a jumble of chaotic thoughts; most of her attention was centered on her senses.

Dan's lips left hers and his body slid downward on hers, sending shivers of delight over her now sensitive skin. He kissed her throat, his lips lingering on the pulse that echoed the pounding of her heart.

Then his mouth moved across her shoulders, down to caress the tender white mounds of her breasts, touching their rosy peaks ever so lightly and drawing them even more erect. "Oh, Dan!" The words were wrung from her. She had not known they were coming.

His mouth left her breasts and moved slowly across the gentle curve of her stomach, leaving a trail of tiny wet kisses until it reached her navel. He planted a kiss there, burying his face momentarily in her softness before he slid still further down. Her heart raced as he continued his kisses, down, down, from the inside of her thigh to the back of her knee, across her calf to her instep, that spot she had not known could be so erotic.

His hands followed his mouth, gentle, warm, knowing just how to touch, how to caress, how to carry her to joyous expectation. And then his mouth began to ascend again. Her breath stuck in her throat as his lips moved upward. She wanted . . . She wanted so badly. But Art had never . . .

Dan's tongue caressed the inside of her knee, moved tenderly upward across the taut skin of her inner thigh and reached her most secret place. Spasms of delight shivered through her and her hands clutched against the sheets. She moaned softly, no longer able to control the writhing of her body or the inarticulate sounds of pleasure that welled out of her throat. How often she had read about this, but never before had she experienced such pleasure.

Then his hard, muscular body was drawn up again and she felt its pressure against her. Again his mouth sought hers, again their tongues mingled.

Her hands clutched on his shoulders, then moved down his back in a pleading motion. "Oh, Dan!" She could barely find the breath to speak.

"Abby, Abby darling." His lips were soft against her ear. "Are you ready for me?"

"Yes, Dan, oh yes!" Her mouth was against his shoulder; she kissed it softly, her breath heavy in her throat. She felt the hard maleness of him seeking entry and she was willing, ready, opening herself to him as woman had for man for thousands of years past.

He was breathing heavily, too; she could hear it against her ear. Then they were joined. She quivered at the joy of it, clasping him to her with all her strength. He moved against her, slowly at first, each stroke a tantalizing prelude for the joy to come. Her body responded, arching upward to meet his, eager, expectant, full of delight.

Slowly he moved, then faster. Her body moved with his. There was no thought on her part; it simply happened that way. They were one being, one entity, and they moved in unison, seeking the perfect moment when their union would be complete—when for a frozen moment in time the two would become one and in that joining share the ultimate ecstasy.

Her hands opened and closed spasmodically and her breath came in great panting gulps. They were close, so close to the beautiful moment of completeness. From deep within her, delight came spilling out in concentric circles until every fiber of her being, every cell in her vibrant body, was awash with delight. It was so good, so beautiful, that tears sprang to her eyes.

Close to her ear came the harsh explosion of

Dan's breath and she knew that the ultimate moment was upon them. In that single moment of ecstasy they were truly one. As he collapsed against her she held him close. This was good, very good; she had been wrong to deny herself this, wrong to think that she could live a life alone, a life without companionship, without intimacy.

7

Abby opened her eyes to a flood of daylight. A glance at the bedside clock showed it was almost noon. She rolled onto her back and stretched luxuriously. She felt very good. There was no denying that.

Dan had certainly made the evening memorable for her, she thought with a sigh. Their first time together had been wonderful, great—and they had made love more than once. In fact, they hadn't returned to Old Vegas until almost three in the morning. Their lovemaking grew even better as they learned each other's likes, learned to adjust to each other.

Under the sheet and light blanket that had kept out the desert-night cold, her breasts began to tingle. If she closed her eyes, she could feel his mouth and his hands on her. Abby rolled sideways, curling up in a ball. Her memory of the previous night was so fresh, so present, that she could almost believe that Dan was there beside her, that any minute he would be reaching for her.

She sighed. He could have been here beside her when she awakened this morning. That had been very clear when he brought her to the doorstep last night. One word from her and he would have stayed. But she had not said that one word, not asked him to share her bed. After a long, reluctant kiss, he had left her to return to his own trailer.

It almost surprised her now—the fact that she had stuck by her resolve—for she remembered clearly the feel of him against her, the need to have him close. But common sense had reared its practical head and loudly asserted that this was the first time she had tried such a thing, and that her career was at stake here in Old Vegas. It was hardly wise to let the whole place know that she and Dan had become lovers.

For one thing, she did not want to be the target of the inevitable romantic speculation. But beyond that she still felt the strictures of the old ways. Better to keep her business to herself.

For a moment she regretted her decision. It would have been marvelous to wake there in the sunlight with him beside her. They could have continued their lovemaking, their joyous lovemaking, right here in her bed. But then everyone would know, the voice of sanity reminded her once more, and she didn't want that.

There was more to this new kind of relationship than she had supposed. She considered it carefully, staring absently at a crack on the trailer wall. In the old days the feelings she had for Dan would have been channeled into marriage; there was no other way for a woman who wanted the world's respect. But today she could do as she pleased and no one would really care. Nor would they think her a "bad" person because she chose to sleep with someone not her husband. Things were not like that any longer. It was freeing, but it was also confusing.

With a sudden flash of insight she realized why she was confused. In the past, the guidelines and rules had always been there. A woman knew the boundaries—and the penalties for stepping over them. It was a rigid system, many times terribly cruel. But it had one outstanding virtue: it remained consistent. A woman always knew exactly where she was.

But today there was no consistent standard, no values that everyone would recognize. Women who were able to silence the voices of indoctrination whispering in their heads made their own values now.

Abby had not been entirely immersed solely in her career all these years. She had been aware that society was changing. But Art had been her childhood sweetheart—her first and only man. Until last night.

She smiled slightly. Dan knew some things that Art had not. But it was not superior technique that had made last night so good. It was that very real sense that Dan was wholly with her. Sometimes with Art she had felt that only his body was present—his mind had been elsewhere. But intimacy with Dan had been more than physical, had been . . . She sought the right words. Well, that was the truth—it had been almost spiritual. Perhaps that had come from her intense perception of his gentleness, his tenderness, his concern for her feelings.

Abby stretched again. It was past time to get up. Way past. Lucky they weren't doing their skit today. Maybe tonight . . .

And then, loud and clear, came the voice out of her head, the voice that represented all the fears and failures of the past. "Wait," it said. "Go slow. You're risking a lot here. You're very likely to get hurt."

And much as she would have liked to ignore it, to welcome Dan to her bed that very moment, Abby felt the voice was right. Caution was called for. Caution and a little forbearance.

When she opened the trailer door half an hour later, she found a note stuck to it with a piece of tape. "Please see me this afternoon at your convenience. Thanks. Jim Seccord."

Well, she thought, she might as well go now. She looked down at her bare legs. She had put on white shorts and a sleeveless jersey in the hope of soaking up a little sun. She knew the workers here wore shorts when they weren't on duty. But she might run into Dan. It seemed silly, of course, considering that he had seen all there was of her to see, but she felt that shorts would make her uncomfortable, or, more accurately, the way he might look at her in them would. She turned back to the closet and pulled out a denim wrap skirt, knotting it around her slim waist.

Then, slipping into her sandals, she started off toward the cantina. The afternoon sun was hot; it felt good on her bare arms. The crowd was light today, she saw. No local school children on holiday, only younger ones vacationing with their parents.

The gritty dust spurted up into her sandals and the sun beat down on her uncovered head. If it were like this in March, she thought absently, it must really be something in July.

The smell of lunch hung in the cantina, but with breakfast just behind her Abby was able to ignore it. She rapped on the door to the office.

"Come in," Jim Seccord's cheerful voice rang out.

Abby pushed open the door.

"Your timing is perfect," said the manager. "Sit down. Dan and I were making some plans. We need your help."

Abby felt the blood rushing to her cheeks. She hadn't wanted to meet Dan like this, with someone else present. She sank into the only empty chair, which in the tiny office was far too close to Dan's. "Good morning, Dan," she said, hoping that her voice sounded normal.

"Good morning, Abby." There was just the right amount of cheerful friendliness in his tone and she silently thanked him for it.

She turned to Jim Seccord. "I found your note."

The manager nodded, pushing his horn-rimmed glasses back up the bridge of his nose. "We're planning a new dramatization. Something a little more ambitious. We want your help."

Abby tried to get a grip on herself. Seeing Dan like that had almost been a shock. Her first unthinking reaction had been to stoop and give him a good-morning kiss. What would Seccord have thought of that? Now she had to concentrate on the conversation and put aside the feelings that were rioting through her. "What can I do?"

"You're a writer." The manager's myopic eyes regarded her shrewdly.

"But I write nonfiction," Abby protested automatically, aware that she was delighted by this chance.

"No sweat." Dan's tone was matter-of-fact. "We're not going to do any actual writing anyway. No dialogue or anything like that. Just a kind of plot outline, something to give the characters an idea of how to behave. They can fill in their own dialogue like we did with the last one."

Abby nodded. "I see." The tiny office suddenly seemed stifling, but it was probably because Dan was so close. She fought her feelings of wanting to reach out and touch him. "Do you have the germ of an idea?"

Seccord nodded. "Yeah. See what you think of it. You tell her, Dan. You're the word man."

A sudden tightening of Dan's lips surprised Abby and she wondered what had caused it, but as he made no comment she let it pass.

"Jim, you're the one with the ideas. Remember that."

Now Abby saw a flicker of something— something close to dismay—pass momentarily over the manager's freckled face.

Dan was speaking again. "There's a stagecoach in working order. We've been keeping it outside the livery stable. We'd like to use it."

"Go on." She forced herself to listen carefully. She could think about Dan later.

"Well, we've got enough horses. We hitch up the stagecoach. Dan and Abby are riding in it. When it reaches the town, Black Bart holds it up. He takes a fancy to Abby and tries to kiss her. Dan knocks him down."

Jim had been deliberately avoiding her eyes as he spoke. Now he met them, but she could not read anything in his.

"We eliminate the other skit, of course," Seccord continued smoothly. "This one will take its place. Well, what do you think of it?"

Thoughts raced riotously through Abby's mind. This would mean no more kisses in public. Was Dan, too, afraid that others would notice? Or was he doing this to protect her? "I—it sounds good. What happens to Bart after you knock him down?"

Dan raised eloquent shoulders. "We've only just begun to talk. What do you suggest?"

She shook her head. "You have to give me time. I can't pick something out of thin air."

"I've got it." Jim Seccord beamed. "Abby can faint and Dan can carry her into the cantina."

"That sounds good." Dan's voice was level. "What do you think, Abby?"

"I-I guess it'll work. But the dust and sand aren't going to be very good for that red velvet dress."

Seccord frowned. "I hadn't thought of that. Well, we'll just give you a different dress. A traveling costume. And a bonnet with a feather." His frown was gone now. "Yes, that's it."

"Do you think a saloon girl would faint if approached by a bandit?" Abby asked. "I mean— saloon girls led rather rough lives."

Seccord mulled this over. "No, I guess she wouldn't. Heck, I liked the fainting part."

"No problem." Dan's smile included them both. "Abby doesn't have to be a saloon girl in this one.

95

Just a settler's wife. I can tone down the Dapper Dan angle and be somebody coming in to settle."

Seccord considered this and nodded. "I like that angle. What about you, Abby?"

She said what was going through her mind and immediately regretted it. "I'll miss wearing that red dress."

"Why don't we alternate performances?" Dan suggested smoothly. "Do the stagecoach one day and the other the next."

"Sounds good to me." Seccord's eyes went to Abby.

She nodded. "I think that would work." Her sense of relief told her that she had been more reluctant than she knew to give up the saloon-girl role.

"Great." Seccord glanced at his watch. "I'll leave it to you to work out the details with Bart. He's got today off, though. You two can hash it over. Now I've got to get to work. Duty calls, you know. See you later."

Abby rose reluctantly. She was loath to leave the safety of the manager's office.

Dan rose with her. "We'll leave you to your labor," he said with a devilish grin that brought an answering one to Seccord's mouth.

Abby stepped out of the office and headed toward the outside door. She did not want the manager to witness her first words with Dan.

Dan's hand on her arm stopped her. "Abby, wait. Where are you rushing off to?"

She paused till he drew up beside her. "How about breakfast?" His eyes held the faintest glimmer of amusement.

"It's lunchtime," she said, trying to quell her sudden nervousness.

Dan grinned. "I know. But for some reason I slept late this morning." His voice dropped to an intimate whisper. "I thought you might have too."

She could not keep back a smile. "I did. But I had breakfast just before I came over here."

He frowned and shook his head. "Foiled again. But listen, my pretty. Come with me to my studio." His attempt at a villainous leer was so funny that she burst into laughter in spite of her feeling of strangeness with him.

Dan ignored the laughter. "Come to my studio, my pretty one. I have something to give you."

"Oh, Dan." She was aware of the nervous quality in her laughter. "Be serious."

He dropped the melodramatic tone. "I am serious, Abby. For one thing, we have to get you outfitted in a new costume. Something suitable for stagecoach travel, shall we say? But better than that—I want you to see what I've done with one of your photos."

Abby couldn't help being intrigued but she tried not to show it. "You put a moustache on it," she suggested as his hand found her elbow and steered her out into the sunshine.

"And deface a work of art? Woman, how dare you contemplate such an atrocity?" He twirled the ends of his moustache and her nervousness faded a little. Why did being with Dan make her feel so good?

"Then tell me what you've done."

He shook his head. "No, you're an impertinent young woman. Therefore, I am going to make you

wait. Besides . . ." His grin broadened. "I want it to
be a surprise."

By this time they had passed Sutler's Store and
were approaching Dan's shop. Abby laughed
again. "Well, if you're going to be that way . . ."

"Turn around," Dan said when they reached the
door. "Stay like that and count to thirty before you
turn and come in. I want to get so I can see your
face. OK?"

"OK." Abby's heart began to pound. What
could be so important—so surprising—that he
went to all this trouble?

At the count of thirty she turned and opened the
door. For some moments she stood stock still. It
was almost like looking in a mirror. Dan's "rogue's
gallery" was gone and in its place stood a full-
length, life-sized photo of Abby.

This was no sepia tone. This was full color. The
red dress shimmered with deceptive softness, her
exposed bosom gleamed whitely. She waited for
that whiteness to move with her breath.

"Dan! It's, it's . . . Words fail me."

He grinned cheerfully. "That's OK. I won't give
you this one, though." His chuckle was low and
warm. "You might have trouble carrying it
around."

"I guess so! But whatever possessed you to do
such a thing?"

Dan shook his head. "Don't know. It just came to
me out of the blue. Call it inspiration."

"Dan, be serious."

He shook his head again. "I did it because I
wanted to. Because you're a beautiful woman."

She was aware that tears lurked somewhere
behind her eyelids. "You're crazy!"

He did not take offense. In fact, he grinned. "Of course I am. So are you. That's what's so wonderful about the whole thing. I'm crazy about you. And you're crazy about me."

"I don't mean like that! Be sensible now. What will people think when they see a thing like that?"

"I thought I might do one of myself." He scratched his ear thoughtfully. "We could use them as advertisements. Maybe let Bart shoot a cardboard me."

"Dan Jenkins, you are incorrigible. This thing is going to be murder to store."

"Not so. It's going to stay right there, I've decided."

He crossed the intervening space and put his arm around her. "Come on, Abby, what is it? You seem different this morning. You've moved away from me."

Her laugh seemed brittle. "Of course I'm different. After last night."

"But I thought . . . I had hoped . . ." He paused as though unable to go on. "What about our friendship?" he asked finally.

"I'm not sure, Dan." She tried to keep her voice from quavering. "I—it was very good. But I need time. Time to think. Time to digest things."

"I understand that, Abby." His smile was strained. "But time is what we haven't got. Remember? This assignment only lasts a short while. Then it'll be over. And so will 'we.' Won't you please let me come to your trailer tonight? Or you come to mine?"

Abby hesitated. Desire warred with fear. She wanted to be with him—she wanted it very much. Right that moment she yearned to move into his arms, to feel the touch of his hands, his mouth. But she had to be sensible, to think this thing through. The feelings she had for him were strong feelings, stronger than she had imagined they could be. She had to be able to handle them.

She turned a little, bringing her face close to his. Her eyes lingered on his lips before she raised them to meet his. "Please, Dan, be patient with me. I just can't. It's too soon. All this—this way of living—it's new to me. I have to go slowly, feel my way. You do understand?"

He stared at her for a moment, his dark eyes warm with passion. Then he sighed. "I want to understand, Abby. But I can't help feeling that we're wasting precious time. Time that can never be recaptured."

"I'm sorry." She genuinely was, but she also knew that she was right. These steps had to be taken slowly.

"All right." He gave his assent reluctantly. "But . . ." With a muffled groan he pulled her into his arms.

She was not really surprised. The sexual tension between them had been growing since the moment she'd entered Jim Seccord's office. She did not try to evade his kiss or the feelings it aroused in her. She knew those feelings now, knew what the result of his kisses could be.

But when he released her mouth, she did not retract her decision. "I've got to work this afternoon," she said.

"I hear you." His tone was gravely courteous. "I don't mean to push you, Abby. I won't again. I promise." He took a deep breath. "Next week on my day off I plan to go the Lost City Museum. They

100

have some artifacts there from the old Pueblo civilization. Will you go along?" He gave her a determined smile. "They have some interesting stuff."

Abby touched his cheek with a light finger. "I'd like that, Dan. Thank you."

"Thank you." He dropped a light kiss on her nose. "Now we'd both better get back to work."

8

~~~~~~~~~~~~~~~~

The next days passed quickly. Abby saw a lot of Dan. They spent several hours discussing the new skit with Bart.

"You know," Bart suggested, "it seems a shame to have the horses hitched up for such a little time. Maybe we should do something else with them."

Abby nodded. "Could you give people rides? The kids, maybe?"

Bart frowned thoughtfully. "Maybe. I'll take it up with the boss."

"Bart can't do it," said Dan. "He's the villain, remember?"

Abby smiled. "Of course. But someone could."

Dan agreed. "Sounds good. Is there someone around who can drive the horses?"

Bart nodded. "Yeah, several guys."

"Then that looks OK."

They returned to the skit then, reviewing how they would do it.

It was midweek when they gave it the first run. Abby, wearing a dress of deep green with a voluminous skirt, a white shirtwaist top and tight, matching green jacket, adjusted the pert bonnet and smiled at herself in the mirror.

She liked this gown. She liked playing this part. When she'd planned this assignment, she'd had no idea that she would be able to act. It didn't really help with the assignment, of course, but it was a lot of fun.

She picked up a small black bag. Dan had certainly been thorough in his outfitting of her. He was a man who could be trusted to do a job right. He was a man who could be trusted. Period.

For instance, he had kept his word about not pushing her. He had been unfailingly polite and kind whenever they met but he had not even touched her since the kiss that morning in his shop. Not even during the shooting skit. Perversely, she was sorry now. She missed his touch—missed it a lot. But he would be touching her in a little while, she thought, as she heard the sound of the approaching stage.

Stepping out, she pulled the trailer door shut behind her. Up on the box sat a young driver, his face wreathed in a grin. Here was a willing addition to the cast, she thought.

Then the stagecoach door opened and Dan stepped out. He was living up to his part. His black frock coat was freshly pressed and his shirt collar and cuffs gleamed whitely. The diamond was missing from his little finger and the garnets from his cuffs showed plain pearl studs instead. His black boots still defied the desert dust, but his hat sat at the correct angle. There was, however, no way to make his moustache jut less jauntily.

His eyes held hers for the briefest moment. Then he spoke softly. "You look lovely, Abby. The dress fits perfectly."

"Thank you." Her voice wanted to stick in her throat. She didn't know why. "You chose it well." She didn't know why she continued, either. "You do everything well." The words were a shock to her; she hadn't known she meant to say them.

She saw the flicker of surprise in his eyes, but he didn't respond to this almost-invitation. She was immediately grateful and her eyes told him so.

He extended his hand. "May I help you in?"

"Yes, thank you."

His fingers were warm and strong around her own and her fingers trembled. But he withdrew his hand as soon as she was safely inside the coach. She felt its absence.

Then he was gracefully climbing in beside her. "All set?" he inquired cheerfully.

Abby nodded. "I think so." She managed a smile. "I didn't plan on a new career when I came here."

"Not nervous, are you?" His voice showed only gentle concern.

"A little," she admitted. "Aren't you?"

He was silent for a moment. "Yes, but not about this."

She didn't pursue the subject. She didn't dare.

"You do remember about our trip tomorrow?" His voice had dropped to a whisper. "To the Lost City Museum?"

Suddenly breathless, Abby nodded. "Yes, I remember."

"You're still planning to go with me?" His eyes revealed his anxiety.

"Yes, Dan."

She saw him relax slightly. "Good. We'll leave around noon, if that's OK."

"It's OK."

The stagecoach started off with a lurch that threw her against Dan suddenly. He caught her quickly, easily. There was one stunned moment when she was certain he would kiss her, but instead he gravely helped her sit erect.

"Thank you, Dan." She straightened her jacket and reached up to feel her hat. By now the stagecoach was moving more smoothly. The driver, though young, apparently did know his business, she thought, as they rolled through the desert around the outside of the stockade and toward the gate that led to the front of the cantina.

The tourists, forewarned by one of the voices that announced the "little dramas," had gathered outside the cantina. They stood in clusters, back out of the way of the stage, parents with young children in hand, older children with eager faces. Abby saw them out of the window as the stage drew to a halt.

Dan opened the door, preceded her out, and turned to help her. She put her hand in the one he offered and stepped down.

"Well, here we are," Dan announced. "What do you think of our new home?"

Abby looked around her, ignoring the staring tourists. "Looks like a nice town," she said. "I hope we'll be happy here."

Dan nodded. "We should be. We won't go back East again. I . . ."

The sound of hooves interrupted this conversation and Black Bart galloped up, pulled his horse to a halt, jumped off and drew his gun. "Hold it," he snarled. "Get 'em up."

Both Abby and Dan registered shock and raised their hands.

"I'll take your valuables, mister," Bart said, indicating Dan's watch and cuff links. For a moment Dan looked as though he might refuse. Then he began to pull out his watch.

Bart moved toward Abby. "And you, little lady, what have you got that's valuable?"

"Nothing." Abby tried to indicate fright. Bart was doing his best to look villainous. She wrung her hands in what she hoped was a typically frightened gesture.

Bart did not move. He stood staring at her and she felt a shiver of distaste run down her spine. They were both getting into the role.

"Nothin' at all?"

Bart's drawl now registered on Dan, who stopped in the act of removing his left cuff link and raised his head.

"Nothing," Abby repeated, injecting a tremor into her voice.

"Then I'll have a kiss." With the gun still in one hand, Bart stepped toward her.

Abby sank limply to the dirt, her eyes closed. The gasp from the audience indicated that her faint had looked authentic, she thought, as her head came to rest on the sandy ground. It wasn't easy to faint realistically, but apparently she had done a good job.

She heard the tussle between Dan and Bart. Then Bart, his gun in the dust, was riding off and Dan was kneeling beside her.

"Abby." The worry in his tone seemed so real. She opened her eyes, put her hand on her head in the prearranged gesture. His face looked worried too. She tried to reassure him with her eyes. Didn't he remember this was all make-believe?

She felt his arms—one under her back, the other under her knees. Then he straightened easily, holding her against his chest.

"I'm all right," she said, as she was supposed to. "I can walk."

"No." Dan shook his head. "I'll carry you inside so you can rest." He moved off.

Secure in his arms, the role playing now over, Abby experienced a welter of emotions. His arms were strong and warm. Her head lay against his chest, the black frock coat smooth against her cheek. She almost thought she could feel the thudding of his heart through shirt, vest and coat. But maybe it was her own she heard—her own heart that had begun pounding the moment he picked her up.

She'd been wanting this. All week she'd been wanting to be held in his arms. To feel the strength of his body against hers. To feel the intimacy and closeness she had experienced that night. And now she was in his arms again.

Oblivious to the crowd of onlookers, Abby could think only of Dan and the next few moments. Would he kiss her before he put her down? She hoped so, she knew that. But it wasn't part of their plan.

The crowd parted to let them through, a few of

the more curious following them inside the cantina. Dan carried her to the door of an empty room and pushed it open with his foot. No one followed them inside.

For a moment he stood, just holding her. She thought fleetingly of his kiss, but then he was setting her on her feet. "It went pretty well, don't you think?"

Abby nodded. She tried to quiet the pounding of her heart. "Yes, I thought so."

"Do you like it better than the other skit?" he asked.

She hesitated. "I . . . don't know." She looked down. "I like the red dress. But I like this one too."

Dan nodded. "It fits a different part of you." He smiled. "You're a perfect woman, Abby."

"Now, Dan . . ."

"No, I mean it." He grinned. "Don't you know that's what every man wants? You're a lady now—an angel. And in the red dress, you're a devil. Every man wants his woman to be both. Only he wants her to be a lady on the street and a devil only in his bedroom."

She felt the color flooding her cheeks again as memories of their night together warmed her body. She leaned toward him involuntarily.

"That's a general observation," he said, taking a step backward toward the door. "But if I don't get out of here, I'm going to get much more specific and forget my promise to you."

He paused, hand on the knob. "I'll pick you up about twelve-thirty tomorrow. Better eat lunch first. Then maybe we can have dinner later. OK?"

He seemed to be holding his breath. She could almost feel his tension in her own body. "Yes, Dan. I'd like that."

"Good. See you later. I better not press my luck." The smile he gave her then was dazzling.

As the door closed behind him Abby sank into an old chair. This deserted storeroom was a good place to think—and she had a lot of thinking to do.

Tomorrow it would be a week, a full week since she and Dan had been to bed together. It was almost two weeks now that she'd been on this job. Another few weeks should finish it.

But in the meantime there was Dan and this new kind of relationship he had proposed to her.

She tried to examine it objectively, if that were possible. First, she was very much attracted to Dan, and he to her. Sex between them was marvelous. Second, completely apart from that, he was great fun to be with—things looked different when she was with him and life seemed brighter somehow. Those two points were both positive.

Of course, he was not the kind of man she would wish to marry. She knew nothing about his background. He could very well be a compulsive gambler. A wastrel. She smiled at the old-fashioned word.

But what did that signify anyway? She was not looking for a life companion. She didn't want to be married. Not now. Not ever. Did it really matter much that she didn't know where he'd been born or if he had brothers or sisters? Or if he'd ever been married? Or what he had done for a living before he came here?

All of that was really immaterial. They had a few weeks to spend together, not much more. A pang of sorrow tugged at her heart. She would be reluctant to leave this place, reluctant, she admitted to herself, to leave Dan. But that part of it was settled. She was leaving. And she was leaving alone. There was no question about that.

The question was—what did she intend to do in the meantime? Did she intend to turn her back on Dan, avoid any more intimacy with him? Would it be any harder to leave him if she kept him at arm's length during the rest of her stay? The answer, she was afraid, was no. If she did that, she would regret it for a long time.

But what if she listened to him and shared her bed with him every night? In the quiet room Abby sighed. That was not the answer either. In a month their lives would become so enmeshed that he would be a part of her every waking moment. She knew this instinctively. To leave him after that would be like another divorce, another heartbreak. The heartbreak she had sworn to avoid.

What, then, was the answer? Maybe a sane, middle road, she told herself. See Dan tomorrow, spend the evening with him, but return to her own bed—alone—before morning. Just see him once a week away from here, alone in a motel room. That way there would not be so many memories to combat.

She recognized that there would be memories, troublesome ones. But on her next assignment she could look for a new friend. She could learn more about herself from him. Wasn't that the whole idea of this kind of relationship? To be open to experience? To change? To growth?

She rose from the chair and straightened her jacket. Time to get back to the trailer. If she were going to spend tomorrow with Dan she'd better do some work this afternoon.

9

<del>~accacacaca~</del>

At twelve the next day, Abby began getting
ready. She had worked through the previous afternoon and evening and risen early that morning to
work some more. The brochure was almost finished, the article almost ready to begin. She was on
schedule, she thought, as she slid into a pair of pale
green slacks and stepped into her sandals. She
pulled on a soft green shirt and reached for the
hairbrush.

Maybe she should put her hair up today. The sun
could be very warm. A flush touched her cheeks as
she remembered Dan's gentle hands taking the
pins from her hair, letting it fall to her shoulders.

She reached for an elastic fastener. She would
simply pull her hair back in a ponytail, a simple
hairstyle to go with her plain outfit. She was
dressing for comfort, not style. Still, she powdered

her eyelids with green eye shadow and drew a pale coral lipstick over her mouth.

She wanted this to be a good day, a glorious day—and evening. Because when it was over she wanted Dan to wait a week for the next one. And he wasn't going to want to do that.

She heard the sound of the Mustang's motor, then his light tap on the door. He was wearing pale brown slacks and a soft orange sport shirt open to the second button. Dark strands of chest hair curled out the opening.

Abby felt desire deep within her. For one wild moment she contemplated forgetting their plans for the day and inviting Dan into the tiny bedroom. Then common sense took over. She had to stick to her guns.

"All ready?" he asked.

Abby took a deep breath. "Yes, I'm ready."

"You look very nice," he said, his eyes glowing warmly.

"Thank you, Dan." She heard the tremor in her voice. It was not of fear, but of desire. She knew that—did Dan?

What was it that made her feel his presence so strongly? she wondered. It was true that he was a very attractive man, with his broad shoulders and dark good looks. They were especially well shown off by his outfit today. She had met other men that were just as attractive, but they had not affected her in this way.

He extended his hand as she came out the door and she found herself taking it naturally. His fingers were warm, sending tremors of desire racing through her. She reached the ground, but his fingers didn't loose their grip. She didn't try to remove her hand. She didn't want to.

The Mustang was shiny and bright. Dan patted the door before he opened it. "I gave her a bath."

"I see. It looks nice."

"In your honor," he said.

Abby felt her cheeks reddening. "Thank you, Dan."

She climbed in the car and he closed the door after her. "Is it far? she asked as he got in his side.

"Not too far. I think you'll enjoy the ride. The desert is beautiful."

"I'm looking forward to the museum. How long has it been there?"

"I don't know. They think some of the artifacts date from before the time of Christ. The desert culture dates from ten thousand years ago. The Anasazi, the 'Ancient Ones,' they're called."

"That long ago." Abby breathed the words with awe.

Dan nodded. "The culture then was called the Basketmaker. They were nomads, living in the open and using natural shelters."

"They were great at making baskets, I take it." Abby smiled.

Dan's answering smile made her go warm all over, and they were only discussing an ancient culture. "Right. They wove fine baskets from willows and yucca plants."

"When did the Pueblo Indians start building their houses of mud?" Abby asked.

"Wattle and daub," Dan replied. "That's what they called it."

"What is wattle?" asked Abby.

"Wattle is the twigs, and daub is the mud they

114

used to hold them together. There are several examples on the museum grounds," he continued. "Built on original foundations. As to your other question, I don't think anyone knows for sure when they began building shelters. The early Basketmaker people were plant gatherers and hunters. Game was good here: deer, rabbit, the big horn and some animals that're now extinct, like the ground sloth and the mammoth." He cast her a sidelong glance. "And lizards."

"Yuck," Abby said forcefully. "Well, to each his own."

"It took skill," Dan said. "Remember, these people used the *atlatl*, a spear thrower. How'd you like to tackle a mammoth with a puny little spear?"

"No thank you."

"The late Basketmaker people, influenced by those to the south of them, began building pit houses. The bow and arrow replaced the *atlatl*. They began to cultivate corn, beans and squash in the swampy bottom lands along the Virgin River."

"A whole culture," Abby said. "Just vanished. What happened to it?"

"No one knows for sure," Dan said. "The people left the valley around 1250 A.D. Maybe famine, maybe drought, maybe disease. Probably they went southeast to Arizona and Mexico. Around 800 A.D. they were at their peak. Dozens of villages scattered along the valley, from Warm Springs to the Virgin River. They grew maize and cotton, mined salt and turquoise, used bone dice to gamble."

"A pretty advanced culture," Abby said, smiling. "Gambling came early to this area."

Dan nodded. "The archaeologists say the remains show the presence of trade, social structure and religion."

"Did they live in the pit houses?" Abby asked.

"We don't know all about them," Dan said. "Some lived in wattle-and-daub houses aboveground and used both surface and subterranean storage. They made finely painted and corrugated pottery."

Abby smiled. "You know a lot."

"You're not the only one with a fixation on the past," he said. "I like to think about these places and the history they've seen. Paiutes came into the area around 1000 A.D. and stayed. Their descendants still live in southern Nevada."

Abby grew silent, her mind filled with tribes of ancient peoples.

"Have you studied Indians before?" Dan asked.

"No, but I think this is fascinating." She turned to him. "I'm so glad you asked me to come."

"I'm glad too, Abby." His voice was a warm caress. His eyes moved over her slowly, gently. She felt her body warm to him.

"I love the museum," he said. "I love the idea of sharing it with you."

"Thank you, Dan." The words were a mere whisper. She was having trouble breathing properly. He was so close and she longed to be in his arms. But that would be later. She must not think about that now. Turning her head, she looked out over the desert.

Mesquite and tumbleweed grew there, with clumps of sagebrush and cactus scattered here and there. A barren land, yet with its own kind of beauty.

There was silence in the Mustang, but it was a pleasant silence. Abby did not feel constrained to break it. In fact, she was enjoying it. It was good to be with someone without feeling the constant need to chatter.

Some time later a clump of cactus caught her eye. She turned to Dan. "Do you know much about cactus?" she asked.

"A little," he replied. "Why?"

"I'm curious about some over there."

The car slowed to a stop. "Where?" He leaned toward her. She felt his breath warm on her ear and was suddenly nervous.

"Over there. To the right." She managed to get the words out without too much quivering in her voice.

"I see. You mean the ones with the pinkish-red flowers?"

"Yes, Dan."

"Those are beavertails," he said. "Look at the shape of them. Looks like a beaver's tail."

"Of course!" Abby's grin was delighted. "They do look like a beaver's tail. How clever." Forgetful of his closeness, she turned swiftly to find his face very near her own. Automatically, she began to turn away again.

"Please, Abby, don't." His voice was soft and warm. "You're so beautiful." He smiled. "You look like a little girl at Christmas with your eyes all lit up like that."

She smiled too. She couldn't help it. "I like to learn new things. Don't you?"

"Of course." His voice fell slightly. "But I most like the things I learn with you, Abby. The world looks different when I'm with you."

Her body began to warm at the look in his eyes and before she knew it the words escaped her. "For me too."

The red really flooded her cheeks then and she tried to hide her face from him. But he was too quick for her. His large hands framed her burning face. "Don't turn away from me, sweet. You've nothing to be ashamed of. So the world is brighter for both of us. We should be glad, not sorry."

His eyes held hers, their look steady. "Shouldn't we?" he urged.

"Yes, Dan." His eyes drew the words from her. "We should."

His lips brushed hers, lightly, gently. They were there and then gone. Perhaps it was best that way, she told herself. She hadn't had time to respond.

Dan's hands left her face and he moved back toward the wheel. "We'd better get going or I'm apt to forget the museum altogether."

She did not respond to this, but returned her attention to the desert outside the car window.

They arrived at the museum some time later. The sun was warm, almost hot, as she stepped out into it. "Whooo," she said. "It must really be hot out here in the summer."

"It is," Dan agreed. "Very hot."

Abby paused, suddenly aware that in summer she would no longer be in Nevada. The thought saddened her.

Dan's fingers closed over hers, almost as if a similar thought had crossed his mind. But if it had, he didn't say so. He pulled her toward the building. "Come on, we've got a lot to see."

She put a smile on her face and followed him. Hand in hand, they wandered among the exhibits, exclaiming over this, conjecturing over that. Like two children, Abby thought, let loose in a toy store.

But she could not deny that she was enjoying herself immensely. She felt alive, happy, bursting with energy—and this feeling came from being with Dan.

They paused before an exhibit. Dan looked down at her. "Petroglyphs. Have you ever seen any before?"

Abby shook her head. "No, tell me about them."

"The Indians carved them on the rocks."

"That one looks like a deer."

"Probably what it's meant to be."

"There's a hand. And that one looks like a barrel cactus. And that one, kind of a lopsided x inside a circle."

Dan's fingers tightened on hers. "No one knows what all of them mean. We should go out to the Valley of Fire. There's a lot of them out there. Maybe next week?" His eyes sought hers.

"I'd like that, Dan. Does anyone know why they made them?"

He shook his head. "Not for sure. They might have had hunting or religious symbolism. You've read about the painting they found on the cave wall in France—or was it in Spain? The one they think might have had some magical meaning to bring in the game?"

She nodded.

"Some of these look like maps or historical records—maybe stories of good hunts. Some might be identifying marks, for clans or people. Some are probably directions for finding watering spots. The only thing the experts agree on is that they can't agree."

Abby laughed, interlacing her fingers through his. "I wish I could go back, that I had a time machine."

"What for?"

"So I could see what it was really like. It would make a marvelous book."

"An archaeology book?"

Abby shook her head, "No, a novel."

"You want to write a novel?"

She chuckled. "Of course. Isn't that what all writers want? To write a really good novel? But this one would be very hard. How could you know what they thought? How they thought? Their culture must have been very differently oriented, don't you think?"

Dan looked thoughtful. "I suppose so. I guess it might be difficult to put oneself in the right frame of mind. Of course, the period does have one advantage."

His comment was serious and so was Abby's question. "What?"

"If you did it wrong, no one would know. Since nothing can be proven, it's all guesswork." He brushed her cheek lightly with his fingers. "Come on, let's go look at the houses."

"They're very small, aren't they?" Abby asked, looking at the row of buildings.

"Yes. Perhaps they were a small people. Of course, they probably did most of their living out of doors. With this kind of weather . . ."

Abby nodded. "Of course, I should have realized. This looks like a storage room, don't you think?"

Dan bent to look in the small window. "Yes, looks like it."

Absently Abby ran a finger over the rough-textured wall. "So this is wattle and daub," she said, giving Dan a grin.

"That it is. And so much for our history lesson." He glanced up at the sky. "I think it's time we headed back to the city for dinner. I have another place in mind. A little more informal, but the food's delicious."

"Where is it?" Abby asked as they turned back toward the Mustang.

"That's the only problem. It's right on the Strip, near the Flamingo Hilton. A Chinese place. They have a dish with chicken and vegetables cooked with cashews that's really great. Kind of a nice atmosphere too."

"That sounds good." Abby smiled up at him. "I don't have anything against the Strip. I just don't find it all that exciting. Gambling doesn't do a thing for me."

"So I've discovered. Funny, some women really love the place. They must have gambling in their blood."

"Not me," Abby replied. "I don't understand it and I don't like it."

Dan nodded. "Well, there's no gambling in this restaurant. It's very quiet."

"I like that." She gave him a slow smile. "You're a very considerate man, Dan."

A look—almost of pain—crossed his face briefly and was gone. "Sometimes I am," he said, "especially where you're concerned."

Abby shook her head. "I think you must be considerate all the time. It seems to be part of your character."

His grin was jaunty. "That just goes to show you how good I am at fooling you." His expression sobered. "Seriously, Abby, you do seem to bring out the best in me."

"No, wait." His raised hand forestalled her objection. "It's true. Why shouldn't I say so?" His hand covered hers briefly and was gone. "That's part of the learning process. Part of the chemistry of bringing two people together. All kinds of beautiful things can happen. Isn't that true?"

"Yes, Dan." She didn't need to say his name, but she liked the sound of it in her mouth, the feel of it on her tongue.

10

The dinner was every bit as delicious as he had promised, the vegetables crisp, the cashews huge and abundant, cooked to perfection in the lightest oil.

"Yum." Abby pushed back her empty plate. "I am stuffed. Absolutely stuffed."

"Good." Dan eyed her over the small teacup. "It's a change from the cantina, anyway."

Abby had to chuckle. "The cantina has very good food. It's just a different kind of place." She picked up the tiny, handleless teacup and sipped the strong hot liquid.

"Anything you say," Dan replied. "But I'll take this place anytime." His eyes grew darker. "For one thing, I can be alone with you here. No one butting in. No one hollering at us or stopping by the table to talk."

Abby nodded. "That's true." She sipped nervously at her tea. All day she had been waiting for the evening, waiting for Dan to ask her what she now saw was coming. She wanted him to ask. Yet she was nervous.

"Abby . . ." His voice had dropped a tone and something tingled down her spine. "Shall I get us a room?"

A sigh trembled in her throat and she swallowed it. "I-I don't know. I want to, Dan. But I'm afraid." She hadn't meant to let those feelings spill out, but now that she had started she couldn't seem to stop. "I'm afraid I'll get too dependent on your company."

Now he would tell her she was being silly, but, to her surprise, he didn't. Instead he nodded. "I understand that. Those are normal feelings. Really. But you'll learn to handle them. When you leave here, you'll find someone else. You'll replace me just as I'll replace you. A beautiful woman like you—you won't have any trouble."

Abby heard the words and she wanted to believe them. If she didn't want the old kind of relationship —and she'd said quite clearly that she didn't—then she would have to learn to live with this new kind. There was no reason why she should deny herself the joy of a good relationship, like the one she had with Dan. Especially if she could contain it, could keep it from growing too all-encompassing.

She smiled at him. "All right, Dan. I want to."

Relief gleamed in his eyes and he reached across the table to take her hand in his. "Thank you, Abby. Thank you."

The gratitude in his voice unnerved her. She

tried for a light tone. "I benefit from this, too, you know."

He smiled briefly. "I know. But I've been so worried all week. Wondering and wondering if you'd refuse me tonight. After last week . . ." His hand tightened on hers. "Last week was wonderful for me. But after what you said . . . I was afraid maybe I was wrong, maybe I didn't . . ."

Abby could hardly believe her ears. How could such an attractive man have so much insecurity about himself? She covered his hand with her own. "No, Dan, last week was wonderful for me too." She looked directly into his dark eyes. It was important that he understand. "That's just the trouble. It was too wonderful."

He stared at her, not comprehending. "I don't get it."

"It was so good it scared me." One part of her mind noted with fleeting amazement that she had never before been this honest with a man. "I've never done anything like this. I've no experience to fall back on. It's all new and strange." She swallowed over a sudden lump. "And I'm afraid."

"Oh, Abby." His voice was husky with emotion. "Don't you know I would never hurt you?"

She shook her head. "It isn't you, Dan, it's me. I have to get used to the rules of the game. It's hard to deal with feelings like this on a temporary basis. It's easier for you; you've done it before."

He seemed about to say something; what, she couldn't tell. Instead he shook his head. "I follow your line of thought, Abby. And I appreciate your being scared. There's just nothing I can do about it."

His eyes darkened and his expression grew more sober. "From what you're saying, it's all inside you. I wish I could help, but I can't."

"I know." His eyes held hers and she felt his concern as a tangible, physical presence. She moistened her suddenly dry lips. "Let's go, Dan, let's get that room."

"OK."

The room was like any Vegas motel room and Abby gave it little notice. Her mind was on Dan. She watched him cross the room and turn the one lamp on low. Then he came back, stopping before her. For one tension-filled second he stared down into her eyes, then he was pulling her hungrily into his arms. His body was warm and strong; she relished the solid feel of it, the good male scent of him.

His kiss was long and tender. To her surprise it held no hint of urgency. It was almost as though, having been given her consent, he wanted to stretch the evening to its longest. His lips caressed hers, softly, gently, his tongue moving tenderly between her softening, parted lips. She felt her knees weakening, felt the curious melting of her bones that occurred whenever he held her.

Her arms were around his neck, her hands buried in the curling hair that brushed his nape, her soft body pressed against his hard one. She felt the straining of her breasts against the thin cotton shirt. She wanted him very much, but she was conscious of the long day, the heat and the dust of the desert still upon her.

When he released her lips, she clung to him

weakly, trying to catch her breath. "Dan." She finally got the word out.

"What is it, Abby?"

"It's been a long day," she whispered. "I feel dusty and dirty. I need a shower."

"I think you're beautiful any way at all," he said, dropping a kiss on her nose. "But I was thinking the same thing about myself." A hint of mischief appeared in his dark eyes. "I've got a great idea. Come on." He grabbed her hand and started toward the bathroom.

"What are you doing?"

"You said you wanted a bath." He stopped them by the bed nearest the bath.

"Yes, but . . ."

"No buts," he replied. "You said you wanted a bath and a bath is what you'll get."

"What I said," Abby reminded him, "was that I wanted a shower."

"Same difference." His grin was contagious. "We can shower if you like, but I think the tub's big enough for two."

"For two?" Abby echoed.

"Sure." His face sobered. "I've been waiting all week for this night. I don't want to lose one precious minute." He grinned again. "If you'd prefer not to share the tub, I'll give you a bath."

For a moment Abby was stunned. She had not even thought of such a thing. Art had never liked anything adventurous or unconventional.

Dan's hands were on her waist, warm and possessive. She slid her hands down from his shoulders, stopping at the top button on his shirt. She didn't know what had come over her, but she liked this new, daring side of herself. "I'll share," she said, her voice soft and seductive. "But there's one condition."

"Anything you say," Dan replied. "Anything."

A little chuckle bubbled up out of her throat. "I get to undress you this time."

"No problem." He bent, his lips nuzzling her ear. "In fact, I thought you'd never ask."

His mouth on the side of her throat sent shivers of desire trembling down her spine. "Oh, Dan." She leaned partly against him as her fingers undid the buttons of his shirt, revealing his hard-muscled chest. She pulled the shirt from his trousers, her fingers lingering in the fine mat of dark hair, feeling the taut flesh underneath. Stripping the shirt from him, she put it on the bed.

Then she knelt at his feet, her ponytail slipping over one shoulder, revealing the sensitive nape of her neck. His fingers touched there, stroking with the lightest of touches and she felt desire deep within her. With trembling fingers she slid the sandals from his feet.

Raising her head, but still on her knees, she reached up to undo the buckle on his belt. Part of her noted that she felt no fear, no embarrassment. It was desire that set her fingers trembling like that, desire that made her want to scramble to her feet and throw herself into his arms. But she remained on her knees until the buckle came undone and his trousers slid to the floor. She hooked her fingers in the elastic of his shorts and pulled them down over his narrow hips. And he was naked before her.

He moved then, taking her clothes from her body with ease and grace. He smiled. "Got any hairpins to do up your hair?"

Abby nodded. "In my bag."

He crossed the room with her as though reluctant to be separated from her for even a moment. She dug in the bag, finding enough loose hairpins at the bottom to pile her hair on top of her head and secure it there.

He stepped behind her as she finished, his dark body in contrast to her pale one. The breath caught in her throat at the sight of them. He bent, his lips brushing her shoulder. "So beautiful," he murmured. Then he grinned. "Are you sure you want a bath?"

Her eyes met his in the mirror and she nodded. There was no hiding the arousal of her body from him. Her breasts were swollen with her need for him, their rosy points thrusting forward. Her eyes were sparkling and her cheeks flushed. She wanted him as much as he wanted her. But that would come. First she wanted the bath, the playfulness, the fun.

"Yes, Dan. I want my bath." She moved toward the bathroom. "Coming?"

It was a rhetorical question since he was right behind her. He turned the water on in the tub, tossed in a washcloth.

"Too bad we don't have any bubbles," Abby said.

Dan shook his head. "Nope, no bubbles. They hide too much."

Abby laughed, a merry sound. She felt very young—and for some strange reason very innocent.

Dan turned off the faucets and opened one of the little cakes of soap. "If my lady would step into her bath . . ." He indicated the big tub.

Abby smiled. "Of course. And will my lord be joining me?"

"Shortly," he replied. "It occurs to me that I can work more effectively from out here."

"Work?" she teased.

"I use the word advisedly," he said with a dry smile. "Since it will be far more pleasure than work." He attempted a serious look. "If my lady will allow me to say so, when I give a bath I really give it. The whole works."

"I see." Accepting his hand, Abby stepped into the tub and settled into its depths. For the merest moment his words had raised a specter of jealousy. With how many women had Dan done this? It wasn't new and different for him as it was for her. But she pushed aside this interfering thought. Jealousy was stupid in a situation such as theirs. Stupid and useless. She let the thought go.

The water was warm and soothing, incredibly sensuous against her skin. But that wasn't just the water, it was the fact that Dan was here, that he was soaping the cloth, that soon he would be touching her.

He began with her face, washing it gently with all the care of a patient mother. Then the cloth slid to her shoulders and neck, moving delicately over these sensitive areas, slipping closer and closer to the breasts that yearned for his touch. Abby almost exclaimed aloud in her impatience to feel his caress, but she managed to restrain herself. Dan knew what he was doing.

He removed the washcloth, soaped it anew. Her flesh tingled as she watched. But he did not wash her waiting breasts; he reached instead for one of her arms, washing it with the strictest attention to detail, his hands warm and tender.

Abby sighed. She loved the feel of his hands on her. Parts of her that had seemed the least erotic began to glow with feeling when his hands reached them.

He touched her shoulder. "Turn a little. Let me do your back."

Obedient, she turned her face to the wall. He used the cloth to run water down her back. "A beautiful back," he said softly. "So graceful. So . . . lovely."

The last was a mere sigh and Abby held her breath. Would his hand—the hand that hovered halfway down the right side of her back—move around to the front to cover the breast that waited? But he mastered his desire and began to soap her back in long delicious strokes that stretched down her spine, down below the water line to the sensitive skin there.

Abby felt herself relaxing, warmth spreading over her body until she felt that all her bones might melt and she would slip below the water. He rinsed her back, scooping up handfuls of water to release on her shoulders.

"If you'll turn again," he murmured. His voice was deep with desire and when she turned she saw his eyes, heavy-lidded, sensuous eyes. They lingered on her breasts, but he still didn't reach out to touch her.

"Now my lady's legs and feet," he said, reaching one brown arm into the soapy water and taking her ankle in his strong dark fingers. He lifted her leg. "My lady has lovely legs too," he whispered.

Abby was far beyond embarrassment. Everything he did seemed right to her, as though it were the ideal thing to do at that moment. Yet she was vaguely aware that if he did something else, it too would be perfect.

She lay back in the water, feeling it lap softly around her breasts as his hand moved over each leg and foot. He moved with incredible slowness, she thought, but in her languor that, too, seemed just right.

Finally he lowered her foot back into the water and sat back on his knees. "And now the best parts."

Abby smiled then, and she felt somehow as though she had just removed the red velvet dress.

He took his time lathering the cloth. He washed her stomach and her ribcage, approaching her breasts with exquisite slowness. But she waited. It hardly mattered where he touched her now. Every cell in her body was sensitized to those strong, dark fingers.

And then the washcloth covered her breasts, swirled around the expectant nipples and was gone. A moan of delight issued from Abby's parted lips. The waiting had made it even better.

When he motioned her to her knees, she had to brace herself with her hands on his bare shoulders as the cloth moved carefully across her stomach. Down, down.

Her head dropped to his shoulder and she clung to him, half in, half out of the tub as tremors raced over her quivering body.

When her trembling had stopped, she grew aware of his hand tenderly stroking the curves of her back. "Do you think I could get a job as a professional bather?" he whispered, his lips against her ear.

"Anywhere," Abby murmured, still clinging to him. "Anytime they'd give you an audition."

His chuckle was warm, his lips caressed her wet neck. She drew back and got carefully to her feet. "Now it's my turn to do the washing," she said.

11

Abby watched him rise and step into the tub before she sank to her knees on the bath mat. His body was beautiful, she thought, like a Greek statue. He turned to smile at her. "I've never had a personal maid before. This will be a real treat."

Her heart soared upward so rapidly that it was a full minute before she was able to recognize how happy that simple statement had made her. It meant that he had not done this before. It meant this was a first for him too.

"I hope my lord will find his servant pleasing," she said in the humblest tone she could manage.

Surprise crossed his face momentarily. After all, he had only jokingly played the role of servant. Her tone implied something else to him, something deeper. She saw that, though she was not sure herself what it implied. She could not be sure because she did not know what had prompted her to enter so completely into this love game.

He was in it too, she saw with a ripple of delight as he made his features suitably stern. "Do a good job, little serving maid, and I will give you a suitable reward."

This last was marred somewhat by the fact that he couldn't prevent himself from breaking into a devilish grin—leaving no doubt in her mind as to what her "reward" was likely to be.

She lathered the washcloth. "If my lord will close his eyes," she said, softly, humbly. He did so.

It was a strangely erotic experience, she thought, as she leaned over the edge of the tub. With his eyes closed she was free to examine his features as closely as she pleased. His nose was very bold, his chin strong and determined. She would remember his face for a long time, she thought, and pushed away the twinge of sadness that thought brought with it.

She paused, considering his moustache. How did one wash a moustache? She didn't know. His hand moved swiftly, covering her breast, and his eyes opened. "What are you dawdling over, wench?"

"I-I don't know how to wash a moustache." His hand on her breast made her long to throw herself against him, but she didn't want to ruin their game.

"It's just hair," he said, his fingers closing over her thrusting nipple. "It washes just like any other part of me. Now get on with it."

"Yes, my lord." Some imp of devilment prompted her to apply the soapy washcloth while his mouth was still open.

He sputtered and frowned in mock anger. "So, you're a saucy one." He leaned toward her, his hands on her upper arms. "You're lacking in respect, my girl."

"Me, my lord?" The humbleness of her tone did not hide the gleam in her eyes.

"Yes, you. But I'll soon fix that. Come here."

Before she quite knew what had happened, he was pulling her wet, slippery body over the edge and into the tub. She fell against him, her breasts sliding down his chest, her legs tangling with his.

One hand kept her against him while the other reached for her chin and tilted her head toward him. "That's better," he said. "Much better. Now, before you finish your job . . ."

His mouth covered hers and delight washed over her. She had been waiting so long for the touch of his lips on hers, so very long. She kissed him back with all the passion that welled from deep within her.

When he lifted his head, they were both breathing heavily. "That's more like it," he said. "That shows a suitable respect. Now, on your knees and finish the job." His eyes gleamed. "And don't take too long about it either."

Shakily, Abby got to her knees, reaching for the cloth. "Yes, my lord." Every fiber of her being called out for the culmination of her desire, but she would play out this little love game because it enhanced the act for both of them.

On her knees, she soaped and rinsed his neck, the hairy mat of his chest, his strong arms and hands. Then she turned, sitting spoon fashion between his knees to do his legs. His hands spanned her waist as she leaned forward to reach his feet. Then he pulled her along the slippery tub, his arms sliding around her waist, till she felt the damp hair of his chest on her back, his manhood pressing against her. His hands reached around to cup her breasts. "Oh, Abby."

Her bones were jelly. She leaned back in his arms, turning her face toward his kisses. They fell on her shoulder, her neck, her cheek, the side of her mouth. She felt herself sinking, melting. It was as if her bones had no substance, no strength. She was just a soft, sensuous mass, his to mold as he pleased.

"I-I haven't washed your back."

His hands left her breasts slowly, reluctantly. "Of course, wench. Finish your job."

She half turned toward him, uncertain how to go about it.

"Get on your knees," he directed. "There, to one side."

She did as he told her, watching as he slid past her to settle in the spot where she had been. Bracing herself with her hands on his shoulders, she settled down into the water again. He passed the cloth back over his shoulder, turning his head to throw her a kiss. "You're doing fine."

She washed his back, full of wonder at the rippling muscles under the dark skin, feeling their strength under her fingers. She traced the line of his spine, vertebra by vertebra, down the length of his back, smiling at the feel of him under her hand. On an impulse she abandoned the cloth, wrapping her arms around his lean waist and pressing her breasts against his back.

"That's enough, wench," he said. "Time for your reward."

"Yes, my lord." She waited as he got to his feet and stepped out onto the mat. He extended a hand to her. It seemed perfectly natural to reach up to take it, to let him draw her to her feet. She stepped out onto the mat—and into his waiting arms.

The breath left her body as his arms went around her. She wondered momentarily if it were really possible to melt completely into another person. At the moment that was her deepest desire.

Wet bodies entwined, he kissed her soundly. Then, while she was still struggling for breath, he swung her easily into his arms.

"Dan!"

But her protest was lost on him. Moving easily, he carried her out into the room to the bed that stood waiting for them.

He set her gently on her feet, one arm still around her, while he pulled back the covers. He turned to her then, but instead of indicating the bed, he drew her once more into his arms. She felt the full length of him against her: the hard, muscular chest with its mat of wet, wiry hair; the flat stomach; the firm thighs pressing against her own. She wound her arms around his neck and lifted her face for his kiss.

But it did not come. "Now, pretty maid," he said, looking down into her eyes. "It's time for your reward."

"Yes, oh yes." The whispered words escaped of their own volition.

In one swift motion he swept her off her feet and laid her on the bed. Then he was beside her. She rolled toward him, needing the feel of his body. His arms folded around her. "What else do you know how to do, little wench?"

She was not sure why he wanted to continue the game, but she was willing. "What does my lord desire?"

His eyes darkened suddenly—with what she could not tell. "I desire that you should please me. Do you know how to please a man?"

She assumed the question was part of the game. "Yes, my lord. If you'll permit me . . ."

He ran a gentle hand up the swell of her hip, across her quivering breast. "You have my permission, little maid."

Abby's hands sought his chest; the mat of wiry hair had dried now. It seemed to caress her sensitive fingertips as she stroked it. She pushed herself to her knees, bending over him to leave wet kisses across his shoulders, up his throat, then down again to his chest.

He moaned softly as her tongue moved on him. She kissed his chest, back and forth across it, moving down the black line of hair to his navel. She kissed that, too, resting her cheek on his flat stomach.

His hand moved to the sensitive nape of her neck, stroking there, then pulled the pins and elastic from her hair so that it fell across his flesh in a dark, soft cloud.

"That's better," he said, burying his hands in her hair. "I love it. So soft. So silky."

She lifted herself and lay across his body, her breasts against his stomach. Then she got to her knees again and continued to rain kisses down his strong thighs, the hair there softer and finer than that on his chest, down over his knee and calf, then up the other leg till she reached his stomach again.

He was breathing more heavily now and so was

she. Carefully, gently, she lowered herself onto him. It felt different being on top. She liked it, liked the freedom of movement it gave her.

She inched herself upward until her tongue could reach his ear. He stirred under her, chuckling softly as her tongue traced his sensitive lobe. His hands spanned her waist; she liked the feel of them there. She kissed his forehead, his ears, his nose and cheeks, his adam's apple, the curve of his chin. The moustache hid his upper lip from her, but she drew her tongue slowly over his bottom one in a motion designed to tease.

There was no response and she repeated the motion, kissing the corners of his mouth. When he tried to return her kiss, she raised her head far enough to avoid his lips.

Once, twice, three times, she did this. The third time his hands came up to bury themselves in her hair. "We'll have no more of that, my pretty." He pulled her head down then and kept it there until he had kissed her quite thoroughly.

She thought that he would release her head then, but he did not. Instead, in one quick motion, he rolled over so that he was on top, her head still cradled in his hands. "Now," he said. "Turnabout is fair play."

Abby's smile grew languorous. "Did I please my lord?" she asked coquettishly.

"Indeed, yes," Dan replied. "You pleased him a great deal. And so will this." And he bent to kiss her neck, her shoulders.

He eased himself downward, his lips caressing her sensitive breasts, sending little tremors of delight over her entire body.

She realized what he was doing now. He was repeating the pattern of her caresses. Down he went, across her breasts to the faint depression of her navel. She felt his moustache against the soft skin of her stomach. Then it went down one thigh, across the sensitive skin to her knee, and down her calf to come up the other leg.

He eased himself on her then and a sigh of contentment escaped her. How could he feel so good? Then his tongue was on her ear, a delicate tracery that set her body to moving against his. He teased her lips as she had his, easing back from her kisses until she locked her hands behind his head in order to pull him down. But he was stronger than she; she could not bring his head down as she wished.

His mouth was scant inches from hers. "Please, Dan," she whispered. "Don't tease me."

His head came down then, his kiss electric, his hands sliding under her back down beyond her waist to press her to him. She was on fire, a pulsing mass of flesh that vibrated to his smallest touch. She twisted against him. "Please, Dan. Now."

He listened. He lifted himself, seeking entry, and she opened to him. It was more than an isolated, physical act. It was primeval, this opening of the feminine to the masculine. She felt it very deeply. She was the eternal female: open, receptive, waiting to be taken.

She had always despised such a description of woman, but now she saw its origins. Lying there beneath him, she felt it in her blood. No matter how a woman might behave in the world, no matter how intelligent or gifted she might be, here, in the right man's arms, her body would betray her into this weak willingness, this heady helplessness. And it would seem very right.

Then they were joined and his body moved upon hers and hers answered it. She felt a surge of wild joy. This was the ultimate experience: woman joined to man in the age-old ritual. Delight gathered in her loins, building and building, until finally it exploded in great waves that spread over her whole trembling body. Her hands grasped convulsively at his shoulders, trying to pull him even closer as she moaned his name. Then his heavy breathing turned to a guttural sound deep in his throat and he collapsed against her.

Abby floated downward. Like a feather, she thought through a haze of joy. So light, so content, until it came to rest on a soft, warm mattress.

Or perhaps it was more like floating in a warm sea. That was it. A warm, soft sea that supported her weight, that bore up a body so languorous that it refused to move, could do nothing but simply lie still.

Gradually their breathing slowed and returned to normal. But when he moved to rise she hugged him tighter. She was reluctant to lose those last moments of peace which were somehow intensified by the warm feel of his body on hers. Even though he was relaxed against her, she welcomed the weight of him. In some strange way it was comforting. She was too content to think any further, noticing only vaguely that she felt a sense of completion such as she had never known before.

After a few more minutes, he rolled over, pulling her with him, his arm keeping her close against him.

"I hate to lose the feel of you," he mumbled. "Thought about you all week. Every night."

"Me too." The words escaped before she realized what they would lead to.

"You wanted me all week?" His tone was skeptical.

"Yes."

"Then why did you put me off?"

She kissed his cheek. "I told you. I was afraid."

"Are you afraid now?" he asked, nuzzling her throat.

"Yes." She could feel desire rising in her again. That frightened her. What kind of need was she unleashing? Some primitive part of her had come to light in these hours with Dan. A primitive, intensely female self that she had not known existed. How much freedom could she give it without losing the self she had always known?

"I don't want you to be afraid of me, Abby." His hands moved in sweet, stirring strokes over the soft contours of her breasts. "Don't think about the future," he whispered, his lips against hers. "We've got now. No matter what we think or promise or hope, now is all we ever have. All anyone ever has. Be with me now, Abby. Share this joy with me."

His moving hands had done their work. Some vague, dizzy part of her brain said there were strong objections to this kind of philosophy. We might never have tomorrow, but if we didn't act as though we would, we might find ourselves in very serious trouble when it did arrive. "Gather ye rosebuds while ye may" had advantages and disadvantages.

There was a certain amount of truth in what he said, though. She didn't want to miss life's joys because she was afraid, because she held back and did not fully experience. And she had decided to give herself this evening.

"Are you with me, Abby? Here and now?"

She moved restlessly under his questing hands, her breath already coming faster. "Yes, Dan. Yes."

"Good." He rolled over, pinning her beneath him again. His eyes gleamed in the dim light. "Oh, Abby, I want you again." He half groaned, half laughed. "And again and again."

She reached up and touched his forehead with tender fingers. "Don't frown. It'll ruin your good looks." She smiled impishly. "I'm sorry to disappoint you," she said. "But I don't see how we can do it more than once—in a moment's time."

He leaned on her, grinning. "But how fortunate that moments keep moving on." He kissed her briefly. "So we can enjoy this moment here and now."

Abby chuckled softly. "And by the time we're rested, we'll have another."

Dan kissed the tip of her nose. "I don't like to waste a moment of it. And so . . ."

His lips moved to her mouth and Abby gave herself up to him. Fully and completely she surrendered her quivering body to this man who knew so well how to satisfy it—and her.

They drove back in the early morning hours in warm, comfortable silence. Abby had never felt so full, so complete, so wonderfully feminine as she did when she half sat, half leaned against him. Almost before she knew it, they had pulled up outside her trailer.

He got out of the car and walked around to open

the door for her. The air was cool and she shivered slightly. "I should have told you to bring a jacket."

"It's all right. I'll be inside soon."

"Abby . . ." He paused and she saw the unasked question in his eyes.

"No, Dan." She kept her voice low. The stillness around them was heavy, almost tangible. She didn't want to wake anyone in the nearby trailers. "I can't ask you in. Please try to understand. I was with you tonight. Fully and completely. But now I've got to be alone."

"Are you afraid that people will talk?" he asked.

"Maybe. I'm not sure."

His eyes grew grave. The moonlight cast dark shadows over his face. "If you're going to live this way, you should have the courage of your convictions. Be proud of who you are."

"I am," she replied. "At least, I have been. But I'm not sure this is me. I need time to be sure."

His eyes turned sad. "Time is the one thing we don't have," he said. "But I don't want to push you, Abby. You have to know what you want." He kissed her lightly on the forehead and smiled ruefully. "Any more than that and you'll have me started again. 'Night."

"Goodnight, Dan. And thank you." Her hands wanted to reach out to him, her body wanted to have one last hug. But she put her hands behind her back and watched him walk back to his car. Only then did she unlock the trailer door and go in to a bedroom that seemed cold and empty—and a bed that had suddenly grown far too big for her body alone.

12

〜〜〜〜〜〜〜〜

Abby watched the days pass. They continued to alternate the skits; one day she was Abby, the saloon girl, and the next she was Abby, the settler's wife. Both of the dramatizations left her unsettled, edgy, wanting Dan with a need so strong it sometimes terrified her.

She knew that he felt it too. The intensity of his kisses during the shooting episodes, the way he carried her during the stagecoach ones, the look in his eyes whenever he saw her—all told her clearly that she had only to say the word and he would be there.

That she did not say it was a measure of her fear—a fear almost as great as her need for him. If she tossed and turned now, wanting him in her bed, wanting to wake with him beside her, it was far better to deny herself. It would help prepare for the day she left this place. The day she left Dan—never to see him again.

It *was* certainly better this way, she kept telling herself. And it was good that she never intended to have a lifetime commitment again. That was courting too much pain. This new way was better, but she was not yet able to embrace it completely. She saw more clearly every day that this was two-sided, like everything in life. It seemed that there could be no joy without the possibility of pain. For joy, by its very nature, presumed the pain that would come at the cessation of that joy.

It was during the nights that these thoughts came to her, during the nights when she wanted Dan so badly. But she stuck by her resolve and he tried to help her—only once asking, with that look of worry that she knew so well, if she would go with him on his next day off, to the Valley of Fire.

She had answered that she would, knowing that she could not put off her need indefinitely, knowing that it would be easier to keep her promise to herself if she knew when she could be with him again.

The days passed and she managed, by disciplining herself sternly, to stick to her work schedule. She knew, of course, that one of the reasons she found the work so difficult was the sure knowledge that its completion meant leaving Old Vegas. Leaving Dan.

She had finished the brochure. Liberally illustrated with Dan's photos, it told something of the origins of the town in 1978 and of the historical significance of the buildings already constructed. She was satisfied with it.

But the article was dragging; she could not seem to get it off the ground. She knew why, of course. She still hadn't found a unifying factor, the something that would hold it together.

The morning of their trip to the desert she woke early and lay smiling in the sunlight. Last night she had slept, slept well and soundly. And tonight she would be with Dan. The memory of the way he had looked at her the day before—the memory of his kiss—stirred her senses and made her body go warm beneath the light covers.

She pushed them back and stretched lazily. Never before had she been so aware of her body, so aware of its soft curves and smooth skin. With Dan's eyes on her, with his hands touching her, she felt herself supremely beautiful—woman personified.

Slowly she got to her feet. She must find something to wear.

An hour later she was ready for their day. She wore white shorts that showed off the new honey color of her skin, and a white sleeveless t-shirt. She piled her hair high, securing it up off her neck with hairpins. They would be in the sun all day and it would be warm. She looked in her jewelry case, then shook her head. There was nothing there she wanted to wear.

She smiled slightly. There was no need for jewelry. That was for making women feel beautiful and attractive. Dan did that for her.

Satisfied with her appearance, she put her shoulder bag on a chair near the door and slid into her sandals, then returned to the table and her notes. There must be some way to pull it all together, some unusual or different slant to make the story more than just a run-of-the-mill piece. But though she stared and stared at the photos nothing would come.

She was still sitting there, chin in her hand, when the sound of a motor announced Dan's arrival. She opened the door before he could knock and hurried down toward him.

He was out of the car and coming toward her. For a minute she thought he would embrace her right there, but he seemed to realize where he was, and he paused. "Hello, Abby."

"Hello, Dan." She moved to the Mustang and he opened the door for her. She sank gratefully into the seat. Her knees were quivering. She clasped her hands together to stop their trembling.

"You look lovely," Dan said as he slid into the driver's seat. "But you always do."

His smile made her body grow warm with the thought of the hours they had spent together, the loving they had done.

She moistened her lips. "You're looking very nice yourself," she replied. His pale blue slacks and open-necked sweatshirt set off his lean, powerful figure. "But you always do."

His laughter was warm and some of her tension lifted. Tonight was a long way off, she told herself. There was an entire, lovely day to be experienced before then and she didn't want to miss a minute of it. Live in the here and now, she reminded herself.

"Did you see the Valley of Fire when you were out here before?" Dan asked.

"I'm not sure." It didn't occur to her to lie to him. "I might have."

He looked at her strangely. "I thought you were here just a year ago."

"I was, but I don't remember much. I was in a state of shock, I guess. Old Vegas was the only place that had meaning for me."

He nodded sympathetically. "It must have been pretty bad."

"It was." Her expression saddened as a wave of old feelings washed over her. "I learned what it means to be stabbed in the back." She shook herself as though the physical action could rid her of the feeling. "But that's all over now. Over and done with."

Dan was silent for several moments. She cast him a curious glance.

"I don't know whether to say this or not." He hesitated. "But I will. Because I care about you as a human being."

She wanted to tell him to stop, not to spoil their day, but her tongue wouldn't move.

"I'm not sure it's over, Abby. I think the scars are still there. Deep scars that keep you from living life to the fullest." His hand covered hers briefly, then returned to the wheel. "I think I'm being objective," he continued. "After all, I don't have anything to gain by your getting over this fear of commitment." He kept his eyes on the road as he went on. "I'm not looking for a 'forever' thing either. Not now. But someday I might."

The silence in the car deepened. There was no sound but the purring of the motor as the Mustang sped along the desert road.

Finally Dan spoke again. "Please, Abby, don't be angry with me."

"I'm not." Surprisingly, this was true. "I'm just thinking about what you said. I suppose you're right. I do have scars, deep ones. But it seems sensible to avoid the fire once you've been burned."

Dan nodded. "Yes, but to carry your analogy further, fires don't just burn. They also warm and comfort."

"Yes," Abby replied. "I know that. And I am getting better, I think. Don't you suppose these things take some time?"

"Yes, I guess they do." He turned to smile at her. "Well, so much for today's sermon. Look, we're almost there."

The road took a turning off into the desert and Abby's eyes widened. The rocks reached skyward, great reddish masses of them. And just ahead of them was a formation that looked for all the world like an elephant stretching his trunk for a drink.

"You should see that with the sun behind it," Dan commented. "It's something you'll never forget."

"I don't think I was here before," Abby said. "I couldn't have forgotten this."

The road twisted and turned, revealing greater formations in the distance: arching bridges of rock, great eroded boulders perching precariously above them. "It's beautiful," Abby breathed. "Breathtaking."

Dan smiled. "I thought you'd enjoy it. There's a place up there to park. We'll get out and walk the trail."

"Yes," Abby replied. "I'd like that."

Soon they were out of the car, the sand trickling into their sandals as they followed the other visitors along the winding trail between the formations.

"Do you know any of the history of this place?" Abby asked.

"Only a little." Dan's arm stole around her waist. "They say it was once a great inland sea, hundreds of feet deep, as wide as a man could see. Except that there were no men about six hundred million years ago."

Abby smiled. "You make a good guide." She liked having his arm around her waist, liked the feel of it.

"Thank you. I do my best. About two hundred million years ago the sea floor slowly rose. Something to do with pressures deep in the earth. Gradually the sea became a desert." He squeezed her waist and grinned down at her. "Very gradually, of course."

She found herself slipping an arm around his waist. "What makes the rocks so red?"

"They think it's caused by ground water percolating through and leeching the oxidized iron. This is sandstone, you know, and it erodes rather easily. They aren't all red, incidentally. Some formations are purple, and some, near the White Domes, are almost white."

Abby shook her head. "It's just amazing." Turning to look back at something they had just passed, she caught the looks on the faces of two young women behind them. Sheer envy, that was what she saw. Envy that she was walking like this with Dan. For a moment she felt a surge of elation that he was hers, that she had a man that many women wanted.

But her elation was short-lived. Dan was only "hers," if she chose to think about it in that way, temporarily. Soon, very soon, their relationship would be over. Then he would be out, walking like this, with some other woman.

She did not like the thought, not at all. But she refused to pursue it further. Certainly she wouldn't want Dan to spend the rest of his life alone. She knew what that was like. Of course he would find someone to replace her. Replace, she thought. It was such a cold, impersonal word—as though she were a thing and not a person.

"Abby." She realized that Dan was talking to her, had talking to her. And not getting an answer.

"Yes, sorry. I was off somewhere in the clouds."

"I want you to see the petroglyphs up there." He pointed to a face of rock some distance off the path.

"Deer," Abby said.

Dan nodded. "That one looks like a serpent."

Abby agreed. "Isn't there something else sort of like petroglyphs? With a similar name?"

Dan frowned thoughtfully. "Do you mean pictographs?"

"Yes, that's it. Are they the same thing?"

"Not exactly," Dan replied. "Petroglyphs are etched into the stone. Pictographs are painted on."

"Oh, I see." She glanced around her once more. "Oh, look. What do the signs say?"

Dan grinned. "Let's go see."

They stopped at the next one. " 'This bush,' " Dan read, " 'is called the burro bush because wild burros and sheep like to eat it.' "

"Makes sense." Abby laughed. " 'And this is desert tea. So named because the Mormons brewed tea from it.' The same Mormons who lived in the stockade that Old Vegas duplicates, I presume."

"I suppose you presume rightly." Dan grinned. "There's creosote around here too. It has yellow flowers."

Abby sighed. "The desert is a wonderful place. Beautiful."

"A lot of people don't think so," Dan said. "They see it as barren and ugly."

"Then they must never have been here," Abby replied, indicating the formations around them with a wide gesture of her free hand.

Dan hugged her. "I suppose it's like anyplace else. Beauty lies in the eye of the beholder."

"I suppose so," Abby agreed. "But I do love it. It's all so . . . grand."

Dan chuckled. "No ladies in long skirts out here."

"No, I guess not."

"Unless the Mouse brought in some captive white women."

"The Mouse?" Abby was intrigued. "Who was he?"

"Mouse? He was a Paiute Indian. An outlaw, they say. Back in the eighteen hundreds he raided around here, settlers and tribesmen both. He came back in here to hide, he had a lot of hideouts. They call this one Mouse's Tank."

"But how could he hide out in here?" Abby asked. "There's no water. And it's so hot!"

"The Tank was a waterhole of a kind. It's really a depression in the rock. It catches and holds rainwater. There are some pretty heavy rainfalls out here."

"I guess this a good place to hide." She looked around at the narrow trail. "You couldn't bring many soldiers in here. They could be ambushed easily."

Dan agreed. "No wonder Mouse thought he had it made. But . . ." He gave her a quick look. "They got him. Whites and Indians tracked him down together. Finally caught up with him near Warm Springs in 1898. And that was the end of him."

" 'Pride goeth before a fall,' huh, Dan?" Abby's grin was saucy.

"Yes." He answered with a grin of his own. "Or so they say."

They followed the trail further till Dan pulled her to a stop again before another rock face carved with petroglyphs. "There," he said. "I wanted you to see the *atlatl* carved here. That's it. The long thing that looks almost like a sword."

"How did it work?" Abby was trying to imagine the Indians, trying to form a picture of them in her mind.

"I'm not really sure."

"The Lost City people . . ." Abby whispered.

"Yes, they didn't live here though. Nothing would grow. But the hunters came here often, tracking the desert big horn."

"They've found artifacts here?" Abby asked.

"Yes. Stone implements used by hunting parties —tools, points, scrapers, choppers, hammerstones. Even some *manos* and *metates*—tools women used for grinding. Probably at hunting camp sites."

Abby tried to envision these women. Lean, dark, silent women. Women who spent their whole lives gathering and cleaning and preparing food. Making clothes from animals' skins. There was no question of equality for those women in the dark past.

Survival took all their labor. There was no time for anything else.

She walked silently for a time, her mind busy with images of the past.

"Abby." Dan's voice called her gently out of her reverie and she realized that she had been walking automatically. She turned to him with a smile. "Off again?" he asked.

She nodded and chuckled. "Yes, I can't seem to help it. Do you suppose I can ever be cured?"

"I sincerely hope not. I like you the way you are." His eyes said even more than his words. "Just the way you are."

13

~~~~~~~~~~~~~~~

The dining room in the Echo Bay Marina was almost deserted. They had lingered over their dinner and now the rays of the setting sun glinted on the water in the bay. Dan reached across the table to take her hand. He held it gently between his and stroked it. "It's been a perfect day, Abby."

She felt the stirring of desire deep within her. It had been dormant all day, waiting like a seed ready to unfurl. But they were far from Vegas. There were no rooms here. Did he mean to go back to Old Vegas? To his room? Or hers?

"For me too, Dan." She looked out over the darkening waters of Lake Mead. "A perfect day."

"And now the sun is setting. It's evening."

She saw the darkening of passion in his eyes and her voice quivered as she echoed him. "Yes, it's evening."

His fingers moved over her sensitive palm. Ripples of desire shivered through her body.

"I thought we might do something different tonight. Find a different place."

Abby nodded, relief flooding through her. Her need for him was great, so great she didn't know if she could stand it much longer. Yet she still didn't want to use the trailer. She wanted to keep this apart, separate from her everyday life. It was her protection, her way of keeping the pain off. This way she was safe. She couldn't be hurt. "Yes, Dan."

He pushed back his chair. "Shall we go?"

His hand in the small of her back guided her toward the door. Abby's lips curved in a smile. She liked it when Dan acted possessive toward her. But of course that wouldn't last. . . . She pushed the thought away and slipped her arm through his. This was now. And she meant to enjoy it.

The sun was just dropping from sight behind a distant row of mountains. Dan paused, his hand moving naturally around her waist. "The Las Vegas Range," he said, indicating the mountains to the west. "The Muddy Mountains are down that way."

Abby smiled. "A picturesque name."

"Yes." He tilted his head and gazed upward. "Look at the sky, Abby, the stars are coming out soon. They seem very close. The desert air is clear."

"Yes." They stood a moment longer, admiring the lovely sunset colors, then moved off toward the Mustang, their steps evenly matched.

The sky was darkening even more as the Mustang pulled away from the parking lot. Abby let her eyes roam over the varicolored desert. This was no simple expanse of barren sand, but a place of rare beauty. One only needed to pause to appreciate it.

They were headed back toward the Valley of Fire and she wondered momentarily if he meant to return there. But the road to the Valley was reached and passed and the Mustang continued on. The desert fell away on each side of the car. The light was failing fast and outside the glowing circle of the headlights the shadows of dusk began to obscure the landscape.

Still she watched. She was not sure why. Actually she would much rather have been looking at Dan, at the strong, handsome face she had come to know so well. But she was nervous again. She wanted the night that lay ahead of them, she wanted it very much. But there was no denying that she was still afraid and unsure of herself. This idea of Dan's *sounded* good. But how did she know it would work? Philosophies could not really be evaluated until they had been tested.

The darkness was complete but the desert around her seemed to be growing lighter. "Full moon tonight," Dan said, pointing through the car window.

Abby looked and caught her breath. An immense golden orb hung low in the sky. The night air was so clear she almost felt she could reach out and touch it. "It's beautiful, Dan."

"A lover's moon," he said softly, his hand reaching for hers. "Just for us."

She returned the pressure of his fingers, keeping them within her own. Yes, they were lovers. The thought seemed strange to her. She had not considered them in that light before. Lovers, she thought, but lovers didn't seem quite right.

It was true that lovers didn't always marry. But often they did. And even if they didn't, the term seemed to indicate some sense of permanency—at least to her.

"Where are we going?" she asked, in an effort to keep this kind of thing out of her mind.

"There's a hot spring," Dan said. "It's way off the beaten path. Beautiful clear water. I want you to see it."

Abby fell silent, imagining a spring in the middle of the desert. Like an oasis.

The Mustang purred along. Soon Dan swung off the main road and the car bumped over ruts and gravel. "It's not the smoothest road in the world," he said, "but that's OK. It keeps people away."

Abby gazed out the window at the moonlit desert. It was beautiful, mysterious and filled with strange shadows. Very unlike the desert in the daylight.

The narrow lane twisted and turned, slowing the car still further. Occasionally Abby glimpsed a shadowed formation, even more impressive in the dim light.

Then Dan took a final curve and stopped. Ahead of them a pool of water shimmered in the moonlight. Waiting only long enough to grab a bag from the back seat, Dan led her toward it.

The pool was small, hardly bigger than an ordinary residential swimming pool, but in the moonlight it seemed unique, from another time or place. "It's lovely." The words came from Abby in an awed whisper.

"Yes." Dan dropped the bag to the ground. Only then did she notice the carpet of grass surrounding the water.

"Shall we take a dip?"

Abby shook her head. "You should have told me. I didn't bring my suit."

Dan smiled. "You don't need one."

"But . . ."

"No buts, Abby. This place is very hidden. No one's going to come here at night."

He smiled and touched her cheek. "Your hair's already up. Just take off your clothes. I've got towels and a blanket in the bag."

Abby stood silent. She was very tempted, but she had never been one to do such daring things.

Dan's fingers stroked her arm. "Just imagine. Pretend you're an Indian maiden coming to meet her lover. The water is waiting, just for us."

Without coaxing any further, he slipped out of his sandals and pulled off his shirt. The moonlight glittered on his bare chest, cast mysterious shadows over the dark planes of his face. He shed his trousers, then his shorts, and stood before her naked. So strong. So male.

Mutely he extended his hands to her and she found herself stripping off her own clothes. In seconds she was naked beside him, shivering slightly in the cool night air.

Then he was taking her hands and leading her to the water's edge. It looked almost too beautiful to disturb, she thought. But he moved into it gently, wading out until it reached their hips. There, with a smile, he sank slowly down until the water reached his neck.

Abby did the same. The whole thing was like a dream, she thought. Fairylike and unreal, this little oasis in the midst of the desert.

The water was smooth against her skin, warm in

contrast to the night air. It lapped gently around her shoulders. In some far-off corner of her mind she knew she should be frightened here in this strange place, in the mysterious moonlight. But there was no fear in her. She trusted Dan.

His hand raised hers to his lips and he kissed it, his tongue tracing the lines of her palm before he released it. She shivered from desire, her body craving his.

His hand made a motion to follow, then he began to do a backstroke, slowly, leisurely, around the pool.

Abby shook her head. She couldn't swim, couldn't follow him. She could only watch as he moved with slow, powerful strokes, cleaving the shimmering water, his dark face shining in the moonlight, full of passion and desire.

Desire coursed through her, heating her blood, making her long for his touch. So strong was the desire that when he reached her side again and rose to his feet, she, too, came erect and stepped fully into his arms.

A sharp intake of her breath echoed over the little pool as she felt his body against hers.

"So long," Dan was saying against her ear. "It's been so long."

"I know." She pressed eagerly against him, needing more. His wet chest hair caressed her breasts. Their nipples were out-thrust, rosy peaks erect against his skin. She felt them there, felt, too, the hard flatness of his stomach. And below that . . .

His arm went around her, clasping her tighter, crushing her to him. She could hardly breathe, but she didn't mind. If there were any way they could get closer, she would want it, would do it.

"Oh Abby, Abby darling," he muttered hoarsely in her ear.

"Dan." Her hands went around his neck, feeling the water dripping from his hair.

"You're my princess," he whispered. "My beautiful Indian princess. Or better yet—a goddess. Yes, that's it. A beautiful goddess. I want to worship you."

He dropped to his knees in the shimmering water and kissed each silken breast as if in homage. Then rising, he took her silently by the hand and led her ashore.

The night air was cooler now. Abby shivered in earnest as he led her up the bank toward his bag. He dropped her hand for a moment in order to pull out a huge white towel. He wrapped her in it, silently, almost reverently.

Then he took a blanket from the bag and spread it on the grassy bank. Gently he led her to the center and dried her, tenderly and carefully.

Abby's body trembled beneath his touch, trembled and grew warm as the blood raced through her. She felt like a pagan goddess, she thought. Warm and beautiful and very, very female.

When he had dried her completely, even to the soles of her feet, he toweled himself quickly, then tossed the towel aside and came to her.

She was lying flat on her back, her body still tingling from his touch. Looking up, she saw him towering over her. The moonlight made his skin glow with a golden light. She knew that body, she thought. And she wanted it. She wanted him.

Her arms opened to him in invitation. Come to me, she willed her eyes to say. Come to me and love me.

And he came. He dropped to his knees beside her prone body. For a long moment he merely looked at her, looked and did nothing else. Yet when his eyes regarded her, she felt almost as though he had touched her, physically caressed her.

Slowly, reverently, he traced the contours of her body. The slope of her shoulder, the swell of her breast, the curve of her hip. He traced each with warm, dark fingers, there in the desert night.

Her flesh yearned upward, ached for those caressing fingers. "Please," she begged. "Please, Dan."

He stretched out beside her and she rolled to face him, their bodies intertwining. "Oh, Abby. All day. All day I've dreamed and waited. I need you, Abby. I need you and I want you. Say you want me."

Her breasts were crushed against him. A sharp stone was digging into her hip, but she hardly noticed it. "I do, Dan. Oh, I want you."

He rolled over then, pinning her to the ground with his hard body. She moved beneath him, loving the feel of him, waiting for him to lift himself, to seek . . .

But suddenly he was on his knees and pulling her up to hers. His lips brushed her shoulder, burning her chilled flesh. Then his arms dragged her closer still, until her breasts grazed the hair on his chest and she felt his hard-muscled thighs pressing against her own. His hands moved along her back, warm and gentle, molding her against him. She clutched his shoulders with trembling fingers.

Her flesh burned now, her blood raced through her veins. She was pagan now. Part of the desert. That dark, secret part of her that Dan had brought to life stirred and flowered.

"The blanket," she whispered, pushing the words between her labored breaths. "It's wrong."

Dan pulled back a little, gazing at her with uncomprehending eyes. "The grass," she panted. "The sand. No blanket."

He got to his feet and helped her up. "Against the earth," he whispered, agreeing with her, and he led her a few paces away.

"Yes." She couldn't talk anymore. Her need for him was overpowering. She kissed him fiercely, possessively, as some pagan princess had kissed her counterpart.

His hands roamed over her, seeking the familiar places, places that turned her bones to water and her thoughts to hazy dreams of ecstasy.

"A pagan goddess," Dan whispered as he looked into her eyes. Then suddenly he was on his knees before her, his dark head bending toward the ground, and she felt the touch of his lips on the arch of her foot. Exultation swept through her, wild and fierce. Thus should a pagan goddess be worshiped.

Amazement struck her then, that such thoughts should come to her. But it was the desert. Magical, mystical—it called to her very blood. Took her back into the past she so loved.

She bent and pulled Dan to his feet. She raised her eyes—living green fires that could consume a man—to his, and saw the blaze of desire there. "Now." She said the single word softly but it carried command.

It was not Abby Holland who stood naked in the golden desert moonlight, but a reincarnation from the past, a primeval femaleness that had taken control of her body.

Dan bent her to the desert until she felt the grass and sand beneath her bare body. He laid her back, there beside the quiet pool, and he possessed her.

It was not a quiet, gentle coupling, but a fierce and savage one. Befitting a pagan goddess, she thought, as his hard body drove against her. And she responded as fiercely, clutching his shoulders, arching upward toward him, the movements of her body as urgent as his. The harsh gasp of his breath against her ear, the pressure of his body against her own, pushed her to new heights of ecstasy.

She was being taken—in the age-old way of men—and yet, in a very real way, she was the one with the power. She knew the heady exultation of being desired, sensed the extremes to which such desire could drive a man—and she was glad to be the object of it.

Then she thought no longer. The desert night exploded with the joy of their union. Delight spread out in concentric circles from the very center of her being. And in the middle of that bliss Dan collapsed against her, his groan of fulfillment the final touch to her glorious delight.

Their breathing slowed, their fevered bodies cooled in the night air, and, finally, with an arm still around her, Dan reached for the blanket and pulled it over them.

14

~~~~~~~~~~~~~

Abby awoke the next morning with her arms around the extra pillow. She had been dreaming about Dan, she realized; her body was warm with the thought of him. She should have asked him in last night—or rather this morning—when they had returned from the desert. If he were here beside her . . .

She loved the way his hair curled around his ears, the habit he had of earnestly wrinkling his forehead when he was thinking, the feel of his moustache against her skin. She loved everything about him.

She sat bolt upright in the narrow bed, the pillow still clutched in her nerveless hands. No! It couldn't be!

But she had to face the truth. She was already more than half in love with Dan Jenkins! Why hadn't she seen this coming? Every time they made love these feelings grew stronger.

Last night, out there on the desert, she had experienced passion that she had not known could exist. And afterward, lying in his arms, looking at the night stars, she had wished this assignment could go on forever.

Stupid, stupid, she told herself harshly. Dan might be able to live this way—to go from one woman to the next with no strain. But she could not.

Leaving him was going to be very difficult, and she had to do it. She had sworn never to let herself in for pain again. Besides, Dan Jenkins was a drifter. A man without ambition. A man who thought only of the present. There was no way to build a future with such a man—even if she were willing to risk another marriage.

This must stop immediately. Despite the sunlight pouring in through the window, she shivered. When he asked her to go out again, she would refuse him. And she would give him no reasons, she thought, her lips setting in a firm line. There would be no talk, no discussion. Dan was far too good at that. She didn't intend to listen to any more of his talk. She couldn't afford to.

She climbed out of bed, recalling the note she'd found stuck on her door when she got in. Jim Seccord wanted everyone present at a 9 A.M. meeting. She would just have time to eat and dress.

People were gathering inside of the Commandant Theatre as Abby walked down the aisle. A quick glance around told her Dan wasn't there yet, and she slipped into a seat between two girls from the Arizona Club.

Cheerful talk went on around her and Abby responded as best she could, but her heart was pounding in her throat and her mouth was dry. Soon Dan would be coming through the door back there. He would not seek her out, not now. But sometime today she would have to face him, have to tell him that they were through. And it was going to be so hard, one of the hardest things she had ever done.

Jim Seccord called the group to order. "Just a brief meeting this morning," he said, glancing around him. "As you know, our new dramatizations have been really successful. Mostly that's due to two people: Dan Jenkins and Abby Holland."

Applause came from the small group. Abby forced herself to smile.

"Yes, sir. Our little dramas have been doing so well we've decided to expand. Going to use the theatre here for a one-act play. And guess who's going to do the writing?"

The blood rushed to Abby's face. She couldn't. She wouldn't. She tried to attract the manager's attention, but he seemed determined not to notice her.

"Yep. Dan and Abby are going to do it. Going to start with the characters we already have, like the sheriff and Black Bart. Now if any of you have ideas for new characters, you be sure to tell Dan or Abby. Either one."

He beamed at them. "Well, that's it for today. I'll let you know more when we get a time schedule set up."

As the staff began to move out Abby sat in confusion. How could she work with Dan on this? Spend so much time with him? It wasn't fair. Jim

Seccord had no right to expect this of her. But, of course, he knew nothing of her relationship with Dan. To him they were just his employees, helping him do a job.

Would Dan get more pay for this? she wondered. He probably didn't make a great deal as the photographer. Was he hoping to get a stake together? To go back to the tables on the Strip?

The theatre was deserted now and Abby got slowly to her feet. She could go to Jim Seccord, refuse to do this. But what kind of excuse could she give? If she said it wasn't part of her job, he would offer her more money. He would probably do that anyway. And if she told him the truth, really told him why she couldn't work with Dan, she would be revealing the very thing she had tried so hard to keep hidden.

There seemed no way out of it. She would have to work with Dan, at least for a few days until she could finish the article. Then she would have a legitimate excuse to leave.

She did not see Dan till late that morning when he knocked on the trailer door. She stepped outside to speak to him. "Hello, Dan." She knew her voice was trembling.

"Hello, Abby." The way he said her name sent warm shivers up her spine. She forced herself to ignore them. "I hear Jim's given us a new job."

"Yes."

He smiled ruefully. "Afraid I didn't make the meeting this morning. I overslept." His eyes frankly caressed her. She felt the heat of them on her flesh. "Last night was extra special."

"I . . . When do you want to work on the play?"

she asked. She couldn't tell him now. There were too many people too close. Someone might hear.

"About six?" he replied. "You want to come to the shop? I have to keep it open, but business is pretty slow then."

Abby thought quickly. The shop was far safer than her trailer. "All right."

His eyes met hers briefly and she saw desire burning there. "I . . . I'm working now. See you later."

Dan nodded. "It's the stagecoach skit today, isn't it?"

"Yes." All morning she'd been trying to figure out some way to get out of doing it, but she couldn't. Unless she was willing to confess her secret to Jim Seccord she would have to go on.

She turned back to the trailer. "Bye."

Seated at the little table once more, she eyed the notes spread out in front of her, the crumpled pieces of paper overflowing the wastebasket. The article simply would not move. Well, she told herself grimly, she was going to get something done this afternoon. She was going to sit right there until she did.

But when Abby rose from her chair to get ready for the skit, she was no nearer to finishing the article than she had been when she first sat down that morning. It simply would not jell.

She barely had time to get into her costume and secure her hair on top of her head, she told herself.

But her mind remained on the article. She had to finish it in order to leave this place. And the sooner the better, she told herself, when she heard the stage approaching.

She met it at the foot of the stairs, reaching out for the door handle before Dan could get down.

He turned in surprise as she clambered in. "I was getting out to help you."

"I . . . I thought we were late." The excuse was feeble, but it was the best she could think of.

Dan reached for his pocket watch and shook his head. "We've got plenty of time."

"My . . . my watch must need cleaning." She was afraid to meet his eyes. What if he saw something in hers—some hint of what she had to tell him? She didn't want to tell him yet, didn't want to have him trying to talk her out of her decision.

Dan sent her a questioning glance, as though he wondered at the way she was acting. Fortunately, the coach pulled up by the front gates and it was time to dismount.

She let Dan help her down—there was no way she could avoid that—but as soon as she could she withdrew her hand from his. Whether he noticed or not, she couldn't tell. She was so nervous she felt actually ill, and she mumbled her way through her lines until the moment came for her to faint.

That was the moment she had been dreading. To feel Dan's arms around her and know that never again would they experience the glory of love. She didn't know if she could bear it.

But she had to, she thought, as he bent to pick her up. She had to bear this pain because if she gave in now—if she let him make love to her again—the pain of leaving him would be even worse.

His arms closed around her and he lifted her easily. She felt the brocade of his vest against her heated cheek, the warmth of his body through his coat. She loved him. She needed him. But she could never let him know it.

She was not strong enough for this new philosophy of his, she thought. Or perhaps it was just Dan himself. Perhaps it would have worked with some other man—a pleasant interlude and a calm farewell. But not with Dan.

Tears welled up behind her closed eyelids and she swallowed hastily. Dan might be able to replace her, but she would never be able to replace him. There was no point in trying.

She would get over this, of course. Just as she had gotten over the divorce.

He was up the stairs now, pushing open the door and setting her on her feet. But his hands remained on her waist, supporting her. "Are you all right, Abby? You look awfully pale. Sound funny, too."

She shook her head. If she told him now she would cry, and she didn't want to walk outside with her eyes all red. "I've got a headache, that's all. The article isn't going well. And I'm awfully tired." That, at least, was the truth.

"You'd better go back to the trailer and take a nap. If you don't feel better by six, we can call if off today." He regarded her with grave concern.

"No, I'll be there. Around six." She saw clearly that the play had to be done—and done soon. Putting it off was too dangerous. She would help him work out the main structure of the play and afterward she would tell him her decision.

He touched her cheek with a brief caress. "You want me to walk back to the trailer with you? You look awfully white."

"I'll be OK. I'll take some aspirin and lie down for a while."

"OK." His eyes were still grave, worried. "Take care of yourself."

She nodded. The treacherous tears were rising again, making speech difficult.

He left and she took a moment to pull herself together. She was a grown woman, not some love-struck teenager, and she would cope with this as she had coped with all the other pain she had felt in her life.

Abby took the aspirin—for a very real headache —and she tried lying on the bed. Neither helped. Finally, in exasperation, she got to her feet and went back to the table. What, what was the missing thread that would draw all this together, that would change a collection of interesting facts to a coherent, well-knit, stimulating article?

By five-thirty she was still no nearer to an answer. She heated a can of soup and ate it without tasting a bite. Then she washed her face, combed her hair and set out for the photo shop. She did not know how she would do it, but she must tell Dan before this night was over.

The shop had no customers, she saw, and she didn't know whether to be glad or sorry. Dan met her with outstretched hands and scrutinized her face. "Are you feeling better?"

"Yes," she lied.

"Sit down over here." He led her to where he had set up a card table and two chairs. "You still don't look well."

"Dan, please!" She barely stopped herself from shouting. "I'm fine. Now let's get to work."

"All right." He pulled out a chair for her. "Jim wants a one-act play. Maybe lasting ten or fifteen minutes, nothing longer. It has to fit into the tour-bus schedules."

Abby nodded, trying to concentrate on what he was saying, trying not to think about what she would soon be telling him.

"He wants to use as many of the regular characters as possible. "The sheriff, his deputy, Black Bart, Hard Rock Pete, the medicine show man . . .'"

"And us."

Dan nodded. "Of course. We're more or less the stars."

She started to tell him that there was no sense in writing a part for her; she wasn't going to be there. But she stopped herself. What did it matter? Some other woman could play the role. Maybe whoever followed her as Dan's companion.

She forced her mind back to the job at hand. "What have you come up with so far?" she asked, picking up the paper and pen, careful not to meet his eyes.

"I thought something about the founding of the town. I hadn't gotten much beyond that."

Abby nodded. Absently she rolled the pen between her fingers. "I heard that the stockade is an exact replica of one built by the Mormons."

Dan smiled. "That's what they say. But here—maybe you'd like to read through this stuff about the old town. Then we can talk."

It was quite dark when the two of them got up from the card table. To her surprise, Abby had managed to concentrate on the job at hand. Only now, when that was finished, did she face the fact that she must tell Dan her decision. Tonight.

"I'll walk you back to your trailer," Dan said.

She did not refuse him. "OK."

He was silent as they moved through the lighted town. She wondered if he sensed something wrong. Well, he would soon know. By the time they reached the trailer her knees felt weak.

She stopped and turned to him just as he took the step which brought her within reach of his arms. She saw the quick look he cast around, and she put her hands on his chest. She couldn't let him kiss her. "No, Dan."

"No one will see." In the darkness his face was shadowy.

"It . . . it isn't that." There was no easy way to do this. She took a deep breath. "I—we're through."

He looked as though someone had hit him. "Through?" he repeated stupidly. "But you're not done with the article."

"No, I'm not. It's just—our 'close relationship' is over. From now on we're friends, nothing more."

"But, Abby . . ." Shock had turned to bewilderment. "I don't understand."

"You don't need to." Thank goodness her voice was steady. "All it takes to end a relationship like ours is either party's decision to do it." She tried to sound crisp and businesslike. "And I've decided."

She swallowed over the lump in her throat. He looked so hurt, so confused. She longed to take him in her arms, to comfort him. "You'll have to go by the rules," she heard herself saying. "That's only fair. You're the one who laid them out."

He gave her a sharp look, started to open his mouth, then snapped it grimly shut as though he didn't trust himself to speak.

"You'd better get someone else to help with the

play, and take my place in the skits. I won't be here much longer."

He stared at her. "But you haven't finished the article."

"I have plenty of material," she said. "I can finish it somewhere else."

His eyes had darkened and his mouth set harshly. "I see." He regarded her steadily. "Good night, Abby."

Then he was gone, striding away through the darkness. She turned and fumbled with the key. It was foolish to cry like this. She would get over him.

15

~~~~~~~~~~~~~~~

She awoke the next morning with red swollen eyes and a feeling of dull heaviness. The sun was shining just as brightly as ever, but for Abby the world was dark.

She spent the morning thinking about the article, only pausing long enough to be sure that Dan had found a replacement for her in the day's skit. He had, she learned from Jim Seccord at lunch, but he would appreciate it if she would watch this afternoon's performance, maybe give the girl a few pointers.

She found it easier to agree than to try to explain why she couldn't. So two o'clock found her on the boardwalk outside the Arizona Club. She stationed herself behind a group of tourists. She did not want to watch and she certainly didn't want Dan or the new girl to see her watching.

Tears filled her eyes as the familiar skit unfolded. She recognized the girl as Nan Sherwood. Evidently she had overcome her former qualms about appearing in public.

Abby's teeth worried her lower lip as Nan helped Dan to his feet and his arm went around her waist. She knew then what she was waiting for. Was Dan going to kiss her? But he didn't, and Abby's pent-up breath came out in a great sigh.

She turned away. What difference would it have made if Dan had kissed the other girl? she asked herself. But there was no rational answer, only a flood of sharp pain.

As soon as she could she returned to the little trailer. It was an unlikely haven, she thought dully, with the unfinished article lying there accusingly. She dropped into a chair and slouched, staring unseeing at the wall.

She loved this place, loved its Old West atmosphere, its recreation of the past. She was glad she had seen it and been a part of it. Too bad every visitor couldn't be a part of it, couldn't feel the magic as she had.

Abby sat bolt upright in the chair. That was it! The excitement of creation propelled her to her feet. That was the connecting thread she'd been looking for. She would use her love of the past, her experience of the make-believe of Old Vegas, to tie the article together. A slight smile curved her lips as she settled at the table and reached for pen and paper. Jim Seccord would chuckle when he found out how really useful her experience had been to her.

Two hours later Abby pushed back the papers,

got up and stretched. She'd done it. The article was finished. All it needed was a little polish. She could do that anywhere.

She glanced at her watch and decided to go to the cantina for dinner. That way she could tell Jim that she was finished. That she'd be leaving—tomorrow.

The cantina was crowded but Abby didn't see the manager. Well, she would eat first, she decided, suddenly aware that she was really hungry. That was the aftermath of her afternoon's work, she knew. She was always hungry after a good writing session.

She selected barbecued chicken and the rest of her dinner and took a table back in a shadowy corner. It was later than Dan usually took his meals, so she probably wouldn't see him. But even if she did, she would soon be gone. Out of sight, out of mind, she told herself firmly, knowing that in this case the old adage would not hold true.

She had almost finished when a peculiar sensation rippled along her skin. Raising her head, she saw Dan crossing the room toward her. He sat down without asking her permission and regarded her earnestly. "I have something to ask you."

She put down her fork. The dessert had lost its taste.

He didn't wait for her to reply. "Abby, will you reconsider?"

She shook her head. "I can't."

"Why not?" His eyes searched hers, looking for answers.

"I just can't."

"That's not good enough for me," he said flatly. "I'm not leaving your side till I get an answer."

Desperately, she said the first thing that came to her mind. "I finished the article this afternoon. I'm leaving tomorrow."

"Then let me have tonight."

"No." It was all she could do to keep from screaming at him—she wanted him so much. But she didn't dare.

"Why not?"

"I . . . I've found someone else." It was a stupid lie, but it was all she could think of.

His face darkened and she began to tremble. Now she had really hurt him. "I don't suppose you'd tell me his name."

"Of course not."

"Of course not," he repeated dully. Then he pushed himself to his feet and turned away.

Not even a goodbye, she thought, as she fought to keep the tears down. Well, at least she had convinced him. He wouldn't be bothering her again.

She looked down at her unfinished dessert and picked up her fork. There was a lot to be done tonight. She'd better eat it.

A merry peal of laughter came from across the room. Surprised, Abby looked up. Dan had joined a table of young women and Nan Sherwood was leaning on his arm, laughing.

Abby put down her fork. She would never get the dessert past the lump in her throat. Pushing back her chair, she made her way toward the stairs. Dan was certainly living by his principles, she thought bitterly. It seemed he had already settled on her successor.

When she reached the trailer, its confines suddenly seemed too small. She needed to move around. Nervously, she set off down the path that led by the other trailers. The sun was setting and the whole desert took on hues of rose and gold, but Abby was oblivious to everything but the pain in her heart.

Laughter echoed through the desert dusk. The same laughter Abby had heard in the cantina. Dan and Nan Sherwood were coming down the path toward her. They were looking into each other's eyes. Suddenly Dan bent and kissed the laughing lips so close to his own.

Pain hit Abby, pain so intense it felt like a physical assault. She stopped, literally paralyzed by the force of it. Then Dan and the girl swung off the path, their arms around each other's waists as they moved off into the desert twilight.

A long minute passed while Abby fought the pain raging through her. She had to get back to the trailer, her dazed mind insisted. Like a hurt animal she needed to crawl out of sight to lick her wounds. Finally she found the strength to make her feet move, to get herself back inside where she threw herself onto the bed and let the tears come.

What she had suspected was true. Dan had already found someone to take her place. But what else could she expect? she asked herself, sobbing into the pillow. After all, he hadn't deceived her. He'd laid it all out for her. She was the one who hadn't stuck by the rules. Not him.

Finally, she undressed and got into bed. She couldn't leave Old Vegas in the middle of the night. She would have to wait until morning. Then she would turn in her brochure copy, give Jim her article to mail, make her goodbyes and leave this place.

The thought made the tears come anew and she let them flow. Might as well do her crying now.

She had slipped, finally, into a fitful doze, when a persistent tapping on the door roused her. Her head was groggy and she squinted, trying to focus on the clock to see the time. It was only around ten, she realized, as she slipped on her robe and knotted it at her waist. Maybe Jim Seccord was calling another meeting for tomorrow.

"Who's there?" she asked.

"It's Dan. Let me in."

"Go away," Abby hissed. "Leave me alone."

"No, Abby. I want to talk to you. And I'm going to stand here all night if I have to."

Abby sighed. She could hear the stubbornness in his tone and she knew he meant it. She couldn't let him stand out there; someone would see him. He might not care, but she did.

With another sigh she opened the door. "All right. Talk."

"Do you want everyone around to hear me?" he asked, glancing around him at the nearby trailers.

"Of course not. Come in."

His bulk seemed to fill the little trailer and she backed away. "What are you doing here anyway?"

"I told you. I want to talk."

His eyes were on her face and she tried to turn away, to put her face in the shadow. But his hands stopped her and pulled her around to face him. "Abby, why have you been crying?"

"I haven't." She knew the lie was useless, but she found herself saying it anyway.

"Don't give me that." His voice grew harsh. "I've got eyes. Now tell me."

She shook her head defiantly. "It's none of your business."

"I'm making it my business." His grip on her arms tightened. "So you've been crying. Did you see me walking with Nan?"

She gave up the futile effort to free herself from his hands. "What you do or who you see is no concern of mine," she declared stoutly.

"Then why were you crying?"

"It has nothing to do with you."

His face told her clearly that he didn't believe her. "Feeling a little jealous, huh? Hurts, doesn't it?"

Abby's anger surfaced. "Hurt?" she cried. "What the hell do you know about hurt? You and your stupid philosophy! You don't know the first thing about hurting!"

His face twisted in a harsh laugh. "Of course not. My wife only ran off with my best friend—but that didn't hurt. Or the fact that I'd just worked myself into a nervous breakdown for her sake."

She stared at him in amazement, this man whose face was etched in lines of bitterness. "But you said . . . you told me . . ."

"I told you what I thought you wouldn't run away from. I hoped . . ." He laughed grimly. "I hoped you'd come to love me as I already loved you. That seemed the only way to get near you."

He pulled her closer. "I was afraid the truth would scare you away. But I lost you anyway." He looked down into her eyes. "I'm not going to hide what I'm feeling. A man has a right to declare himself, even if he hasn't got a chance."

He shook her lightly. "I love you, Abby Holland.

Not just for this moment. I want to love you forever. Forever! Do you hear?"

Dumbly she stared at him. How could this be possible? What happened to what he'd told her? All that philosophy?

"Now you can go back to your new man," he said grimly. "But first, for old time's sake . . ."

He pulled her roughly into his arms and his mouth covered hers. It was a punishing kiss, savage in its intensity. But it did not frighten her. She responded to it eagerly, struggling to free her arms so she could get them around his neck.

He loosened his hold on her and held her at arm's length. "What the devil's going on?" he demanded.

"Oh, Dan, Dan!" Joy threatened to make her inarticulate. Her kisses covered his face. "I love you! I love you."

"You do?" Shock kept him silent for several seconds. Then he grabbed her in a great bear hug and swung her around and around. "You love me!"

"Dan, Dan darling! There's not enough room in here!"

"Abby! Abby!" He claimed her lips again for a long satisfying kiss. When it was finished, he released her mouth but kept her in his arms. "Will you marry me, Abby Holland?"

"Oh Dan, I do love you. But . . . but I don't know anything about you." The thought of losing him now was almost more than she could bear, but she had to know. "Do . . . do you gamble?"

"No, Abby. I find it boring." He regarded her gravely. "Why do you ask?"

"I . . . I can't help wondering why you're here."

Dan frowned. "I've been keeping my identity a secret."

She tried to still the pounding of her heart. Had he done something terrible? "What do you mean?"

He laughed. "Relax, sweetheart. I haven't done anything wrong, if that's what you're worrying about. I'm a writer."

"A writer!" Abby echoed incredulously.

"Yep. My name is Dan Jenkins, but I write under the name of Jenkins Daniels."

"Mysteries!" Abby cried. "You write mysteries."

"That's right, honey." He kissed the tip of her nose. "My wife ran away with my best friend. She said I didn't spend enough time with her. She also said I didn't make enough money. I was working like crazy to get her the things she wanted. And then she split. I came that close to a breakdown." He held his finger and thumb half an inch apart. "Nervous exhaustion, the doctor said. He told me to get away, not to write anything for six months. Jim Seccord had gone to school with me. When he found out what had happened, he invited me down here. We used to be into photography together, so he asked me to run the shop. Something to keep me busy until I could get back to writing."

She reached up to kiss his chin, temporarily interrupting his story.

He smiled. "Actually, my six months were up the week you got here—but I couldn't leave after I saw you. I knew, you see. I knew the moment I saw you that we were destined for each other."

"Oh, Dan." She wrapped her arms around him and hugged him tight. "You're a writer too."

But then a voice from the past found its tongue.

"My career," she stammered. "My work. I can't give up my work." She dropped her eyes to his chest.

His hand under her chin tilted it upward till his eyes again met hers, dark, serious eyes. "Silly Abby. I know all about you, remember? I couldn't ask you to give up your career." He smiled impishly. "You won't ask me to give up mine, will you?"

For a moment she took his question at face value, then she broke into laughter. "Of course not, my darling. Oh, it's going to be wonderful, just wonderful. We can travel together. We can work together. . . ."

Dan's finger on her lips silenced her. "Speaking of together . . ." He swung her up in his arms. "How about sleeping together? When can we start that?"

Nestling her head into the crook of his shoulder, she used her free hand to undo his top button. "How about right now?" she asked seductively.

"Now," he repeated. "That sounds good. We won't forget the past, Abby. We'll change. We'll grow. But we'll do it together. Promise?"

"I promise," she replied solemnly, but her joy could not be suppressed. "Oh, Dan, please don't keep me waiting any longer. Give me this moment's time. Now."

"I will, my love. I will." And they moved off together toward the bedroom.

Genuine Silhouette sterling silver bookmark for only $15.95!

What a beautiful way to hold your place in your current romance! This genuine sterling silver bookmark, with the distinctive Silhouette symbol in elegant black, measures 1½" long and 1" wide. It makes a beautiful gift for yourself, and for every romantic you know! And, at only $15.95 each, including all postage and handling charges, you'll want to order several now, while supplies last.

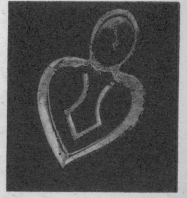

Send your name and address with check or money order for $15.95 per bookmark ordered to
Simon & Schuster Enterprises
120 Brighton Rd., P.O. Box 5020
Clifton, N.J. 07012
Attn: Bookmark

Bookmarks can be ordered pre-paid only. No charges will be accepted. Please allow 4-6 weeks for delivery.

YOU'LL BE SWEPT AWAY
WITH SILHOUETTE DESIRE

$1.75 each

1 ☐ CORPORATE AFFAIR
James

2 ☐ LOVE'S SILVER WEB
Monet

3 ☐ WISE FOLLY
Clay

4 ☐ KISS AND TELL
Carey

5 ☐ WHEN LAST WE LOVED
Baker

6 ☐ A FRENCHMAN'S KISS
Mallory

7 ☐ NOT EVEN FOR LOVE
St. Claire

8 ☐ MAKE NO PROMISES
Dee

9 ☐ MOMENT IN TIME
Simms

10 ☐ WHENEVER I LOVE YOU
Smith

$1.95 each

11 ☐ VELVET TOUCH
James

12 ☐ THE COWBOY AND THE
LADY Palmer

13 ☐ COME BACK, MY LOVE
Wallace

14 ☐ BLANKET OF STARS
Valley

15 ☐ SWEET BONDAGE
Vernon

16 ☐ DREAM COME TRUE
Major

17 ☐ OF PASSION BORN
Simms

18 ☐ SECOND HARVEST
Ross

19 ☐ LOVER IN PURSUIT
James

20 ☐ KING OF DIAMONDS
Allison

21 ☐ LOVE INTHE CHINA SEA
Baker

22 ☐ BITTERSWEET IN BERN
Durant

23 ☐ CONSTANT STRANGER
Sunshine

24 ☐ SHARED MOMENTS
Baxter

25 ☐ RENAISSANCE MAN
James

26 ☐ SEPTEMBER MORNING
Palmer

27 ☐ ON WINGS OF NIGHT
Conrad

28 ☐ PASSIONATE JOURNEY
Lovan

29 ☐ ENCHANTED DESERT
Michelle

30 ☐ PAST FORGETTING
Lind

31 ☐ RECKLESS PASSION
James

32 ☐ YESTERDAY'S DREAMS
Clay

38 ☐ SWEET SERENITY
Douglass

39 ☐ SHADOW OF BETRAYAL
Monet

40 ☐ GENTLE CONQUEST
Mallory

41 ☐ SEDUCTION BY DESIGN
St. Claire

42 ☐ ASK ME NO SECRETS
Stewart

43 ☐ A WILD, SWEET MAGIC
Simms

44 ☐ HEART OVER MIND West

45 ☐ EXPERIMENT IN LOVE Clay

46 ☐ HER GOLDEN EYES Chance

47 ☐ SILVER PROMISES Michelle

48 ☐ DREAM OF THE WEST
Powers

49 ☐ AFFAIR OF HONOR James

Silhouette Desire

50 ☐ FRIENDS AND LOVERS Palmer	68 ☐ SHADOW OF YESTERDAY Browning
51 ☐ SHADOW OF THE MOUNTAIN Lind	69 ☐ PASSION'S PORTRAIT Carey
52 ☐ EMBERS OF THE SUN Morgan	70 ☐ DINNER FOR TWO Victor
53 ☐ WINTER LADY Joyce	71 ☐ MAN OF THE HOUSE Joyce
54 ☐ IF EVER YOU NEED ME Fulford	72 ☐ NOBODY'S BABY Hart
55 ☐ TO TAME THE HUNTER James	73 ☐ A KISS REMEMBERED St. Claire
56 ☐ FLIP SIDE OF YESTERDAY Douglass	74 ☐ BEYOND FANTASY Douglass
57 ☐ NO PLACE FOR A WOMAN Michelle	75 ☐ CHASE THE CLOUDS McKenna
58 ☐ ONE NIGHT'S DECEPTION Mallory	76 ☐ STORMY SERENADE Michelle
59 ☐ TIME STANDS STILL Powers	77 ☐ SUMMER THUNDER Lowell
60 ☐ BETWEEN THE LINES Dennis	78 ☐ BLUEPRINT FOR RAPTURE Barber
61 ☐ ALL THE NIGHT LONG Simms	79 ☐ SO SWEET A MADNESS Simms
62 ☐ PASSIONATE SILENCE Monet	80 ☐ FIRE AND ICE Palmer
63 ☐ SHARE YOUR TOMORROWS Dee	81 ☐ OPENING BID Kennedy
64 ☐ SONATINA Milan	82 ☐ SUMMER SONG Clay
65 ☐ RECKLESS VENTURE Allison	83 ☐ HOME AT LAST Chance
66 ☐ THE FIERCE GENTLENESS Langtry	84 ☐ IN A MOMENT'S TIME Powers
67 ☐ GAMEMASTER James	

SILHOUETTE DESIRE, Department SD/6
1230 Avenue of the Americas
New York, NY 10020

Please send me the books I have checked above. I am enclosing $_____
(please add 50¢ to cover postage and handling. NYS and NYC residents please add
appropriate sales tax.) Send check or money order—no cash or C.O.D.'s please.
Allow six weeks for delivery.

NAME _____

ADDRESS _____

CITY _____ STATE/ZIP _____

Get 6 new Silhouette Special Editions every month for a 15-day FREE trial!

Free Home Delivery, Free Previews, Free Bonus Books. Silhouette Special Editions are a new kind of romance novel. These are big, powerful stories that will capture your imagination. They're longer, with fully developed characters and intricate plots that will hold you spellbound from the first page to the very last.

Each month we will send you six exciting *new* Silhouette Special Editions, just as soon as they are published. If you enjoy them as much as we think you will, pay the invoice enclosed with your shipment. **They're delivered right to your door with never a charge for postage or handling, and there's no obligation to buy anything at any time.** To start receiving Silhouette Special Editions regularly, mail the coupon below today.

Silhouette Special Edition